Arryn

MYSTIC PROTECTORS SERIES BOOK 4

KATHI S. BARTON

WCP

World Castle Publishing, LLC
Pensacola, Florida

Copyright © Kathi S. Barton 2015
Print ISBN: 9781629892207
eBook ISBN: 9781629892214
First Edition World Castle Publishing, LLC, February 20, 2015
http://www.worldcastlepublishing.com

Licensing Notes

Cover: Karen Fuller
Editor: Maxine Bringenberg

Chapter 1

Boss watched the play between the men. It was something that He enjoyed more than He could have told anyone. Not that anyone wouldn't have believed Him, but He doubted that they'd get it. He rarely had time to do much more than work and this was a treat, a rare one that He wanted to enjoy. When Kala sat beside Him, He nearly told her that He preferred to be alone, but knew that she'd stay anyway.

"She's here." Boss knew that so said nothing, but looked at her. "You said she was lost, but you never said that she was...what happened to her?"

"It will be her story to tell and not mine, I'm afraid. There is little I can tell you that you'd believe anyway. It is a story that hurts my heart." Kala nodded and He turned back to the fields where the other protectors were. "You have sent her to see Judith, as I have asked you to do?"

"I have. She's not overly thrilled about it, but she went. What can Judith do for her that we can't?" Boss didn't answer. "You said she's wholly human, but she's not, is she?"

"No. She's human but not...." He stood up then and so did Kala. She was large with her and Riss's children now, and He was going to have to have her rest soon. But she would fight Him on this, as she did everything. "Judith can see what others cannot. What the girl might not even be aware of. And what she is aware of has her hurting in ways that no one can heal but herself."

Reyna Sharp was weighing heavily on His mind and heart. He was sure that everyone around Him could see that He was in pain, but not the reason for it. Michael might have an idea, but he'd never breach his promise to keep things he knew to himself. It was one of the many things that He loved about the man. And He was fearful that her mate would not be able to break through her pain to help her in time.

"Is she for Arryn?" Boss said nothing, but He had a feeling that Kala knew a great deal more than anyone. Judith and she could see right into the heart and mind of anyone. "She's hard. Hurt and hard. I think she might be harder than even Judith or I were before You helped us with our truer nature. Not like Dusty, but maybe close."

"I don't know if perhaps we'll be too late for her." Kala said His name and He turned to look at her. "I have found her to be unwilling to accept things. And there were things that she has been told that I wasn't aware of until a few days ago. The one person that should have loved her more than herself has betrayed her in ways that…I wish I could have been made aware of it sooner."

"Is she going to die?" Boss nodded at Kala's question. "How? And I'm assuming You mean her mother. What could a mother do to her own child that has hurt You so badly? And if You tell me it was in the name of what her future holds, I won't believe You. You're hurting too."

Boss needed to talk. And in talking with this woman, His first of many wives of His protectors, He knew that she'd not judge Him. Perhaps she'd be angry with Him for a time, but she'd not be that way for long. As He stood there, Boss thought of the day that Reyna had been born.

"She was born of rape. Her mother had been brutalized and Reyna was conceived. It was never known to the people who cared for her which man had sired her. There had been so many." Kala asked Him if He knew. "It was them all. She is a product of all of them."

"And these men, did they live or have they paid for their crime against her mother?" Boss told her that they had not. "I see. And you are expecting her to take care of this for You? To bring these men to justice for You?"

"Nay, I do not see them playing a part in her life again. They do not...two of them know of her but they care nothing for her, and will not come into her life for any reason. The rest have no knowledge of her birth or her life." Kala asked Him how many there had been. "Five. Three of them aren't human, but that mattered little in the outcome. Their magic — some semi-powerful, some not — has become a part of the girl. It gave her a talent that I thought we could use here."

"Yet you said that she's human. I'm assuming that there is a difference with this that I don't understand." He told Kala that there was much she did not understand. "Yet you want me to help her."

"I want you to care for her. Keep her from harm." He turned to her then. "She is for Arryn as you have surmised, but he will...I fear that he will be hurt more from this child than by anything he did in his long life. She will not mean it, but he will be hurt by her...if things do not change."

"You told us that she was lost. I guess I don't understand that. What does her being lost mean to You?"

He turned away again; the pain in His own heart hurt. "Boss? I can't help her if You don't tell me."

"Her soul is no longer hers and she belongs to the underworld. A deal was made for it long before I was made aware of it. She has...I have failed her in this." He turned to Kala to tell her the rest. "In a few weeks she will be taken to the underworld as a plaything. And once there, everything will be lost for her."

"Who does she belong to?" He only looked at her and Kala knew. "We'll get it back for her. Who would do such a thing? How could it be done?"

"Her mother, as you have guessed." Kala sat down then. Her babies moved beneath her hand and Boss moved to put His hand there as well...to calm them, He told Himself, but it was for His comfort. "She gave her daughter to him when she was but a babe, still needing the bottle to feed. Her life—her mother's life—was not a hard one, but her mind was not always calm after what they did to her. In a fit of...what I can only think of as madness, she sold her child to him in order to live forever. It has not served her as she'd hoped, I think."

"Is there a way to get it back for her?" There was a way, but He wasn't willing to speak of it yet. "Boss, You do know that once Arryn finds out what she is to him, he will do everything in his power to get it back for her."

"I know this as well as you do." He moved away from her now. "I would ask that you say nothing of this for now. I have things I must work out that only I can deal with. Should you talk to her again, watch her closely. Her magic, that of her sires, is coming to fruition and she will need help with it. I think she can control it, but there are times when she will be overwhelmed by it, too." Kala nodded and Boss willed Himself to His office.

The pictures on His wall today were not ones that He normally held there. Images of the violent rape of Penny Sharp, mother to Reyna, were there for Him to see and to watch again and again. And He had, over and over, looking for a clue He knew was there. He'd not been able to find it, even after all these years, and not...well, now it was nearly too late to do much about it.

"You have spoken to Kala then?" Boss looked up at Michael...not only His right hand man, but His friend as well. When He nodded, Michael came into the room and sat down in the chair that had seated so many before today. "She will do much to help her. I think perhaps you should tell the others what You think as well. They can help You where no one else would."

"I cannot tell them what I do not know for sure." Michael nodded and said nothing more as He continued. "Her mother was not just in the wrong place at the wrong time, my friend, but someone planned this. There is something there that I am missing."

"I believe You. But like You have said before, we cannot prove it so we must keep digging. The things in the underworld are not as easy for us to see, even when we know something has been done to one so young. How much time does she have left?" Boss knew right to the second, and didn't look at the clock ticking down on the wall as He told Michael. "So little left."

"I'm aware of that." He looked at Michael. "I'm sorry, but I feel as if I have failed her. It was all I could do not to go to the girl and tell her how sorry I am for what I failed to do for her. I know not what to do, other than to have Arryn love her for what little time she has left."

After Michael left him, Boss looked at the wall of frames again. He watched the images move forward, and feared that one outcome in particular would be the one that happened. The second one, this one more pleasing to Him, was something He only watched when in His deepest despair. That one not only had Arryn happy, but young Reyna whole as well. And with a family to love.

He reached for Reyna now, and saw that she was just arriving at the shop that Judith owned. He was happy to see that not only was Dusty there, but young Kip as well. He was very proud of the young boy, almost as much as He was of Kip's new mother. As he moved closer to them in the shop, He listened for any sign that Reyna was going to be friendly towards the others, or whether she would remain as she'd been her entire life…alone.

~~~

Reyna, or Renie to most people who knew her, walked into the shop and asked to speak to a woman by the name of Judith. Renie knew that Judith was the owner of the place, but not what the hell she was doing there. But the presence…the feeling that they were not alone made her look around. It was then that a young man came to ask her if she was ready to be seated.

"I'm here to see a Judith Guardian." He nodded but watched her. There was something about the young kid that made her squirm a little. "Are you going to draw a picture later or are you always this rude?"

"No. Rude would be what you are right now. I'm just trying to see what you have going on in your hair. Did you know that you have about ten shades of red going on there?" Renie lifted her chin and the kid laughed. "Yeah, that'll get you far in life. I had the same attitude a while back. Got me nowhere but stuck with a demon that wanted to fuck me. What's your excuse?"

"I want to be left alone." Which was true. Renie had no use for people and would really like to be left alone. When the boy showed her to the table near the counter and left her, Renie looked around.

The hum of the computers around the room comforted her. She could have pulled her own out and lost herself in it, but the courts had told her that she wasn't allowed to use it unless it was for business. There were ways for her to get around that, but for now she'd follow their rules. When a very beautiful woman came toward her Renie started to stand up, but she just stayed where she was. There was nothing these people could give her that she couldn't buy on her own.

"You're Reyna Sharp." Renie nodded and told her to call her Renie. "Okay. I've been told that you can work on my systems for me. Get me up and running faster than anyone in town, as well as keep the place safe for people to use the Wi-Fi. And to also find out why I'm losing money hand over fist in the bank. They have no idea either. I checked."

"I can do that. But you know that I'm here only because I broke the law." Judith asked her what she'd done. "I didn't take anything, but only pointed out the error of their ways."

"You broke into their server and made it fuck up for an entire week. Then you sent an email to them and told them how to fix it. I believe that is the only reason you're not in prison. Cyber-espionage is against the law, as I'm sure you've figured out." Renie said nothing. She knew it was wrong before she'd done it, but she'd been bored and hurt, which usually got her into trouble. "How old are you? You don't look to be much older than Kip."

"I'm almost twenty-five. I'm just undernourished, the doc said, as well as I don't get enough outside activity. Like that is supposed to be a diagnosis." Judith said that she thought it was. "I'm fine. I have to work for you for six months. But I'm also to tell you that I don't have that long."

"What do you mean?" Renie looked away. "I can look if you don't tell me. I have that ability to see what others might keep from me."

"I'm going to hell." When she stood up so did Judith. If she understood what was going to happen to her, she didn't say. Renie asked her where she wanted her to go to work.

"Here or in the office. I know from Kala that you want to be left alone, so if you go to the office, it'll be noisy and crowded. If you pick a table, no one will bother you. What do you need from me?" Renie told her. "All right. I'm assuming that you are aware that by me giving you my passwords that if anything comes up missing, I will own your ass and make your trip to hell seem like child's play."

"Bring it on." Renie stared at the woman, who finally nodded and walked away. Judith had been in her mind, and while Renie knew that she could have stopped her from looking, she didn't bother. There were only five more months of her life left as far as anyone knew, and she was tired of thinking about it all the time. In fact, if asked she'd tell them she was simply tired.

As soon as she sat at one of the bigger tables in the pretty little restaurant, Renie pulled out her computers and other things she'd need. The password and account numbers were brought to her, as well as a thick sandwich. Renie ate half of it and drank two of the bottles of water before wrapping up what was left and putting it in her bag with the last of the water. She had no idea when she'd take time for another meal like this one.

It took her less than five minutes to access all the accounts, and another five to get into some that Judith hadn't given her. There was a great deal of money in the accounts, five of them that she'd found already, as well as her business and savings accounts. The woman had to be doing a hell of a job if her balance was any indication. When another bottle of water was put next to her, Renie opened it with a thanks but never looked up.

She was vaguely aware of people coming and going in the place. There were noises that made her think that a bunch of good friends were there. Laughter as well as the feeling of love entered into her head. Renie was aware of it all but never looked up. Her mind was nearly completely focused on what she was doing.

"You having any troubles?" Renie looked up when someone touched her on her hand. Jerking back from the man, she watched as he took a step back from her. "I'm sorry. I didn't mean to scare you."

"You didn't." He nodded but said nothing more as he sat down. "I don't want any company, thanks. I'm here to work."

"I was to tell you that there is an apartment upstairs that you can use while you're here. It's part of the deal that we made with the systems that brought you here." Renie didn't show how excited she was about a place to stay, but stared at the man. "I'm Agon; Judith is my wife."

"Good for you." He smiled at her and she thought of flowers in the spring. Shoving such a stupid thought out of her head, she snapped at him. "I'm really busy here. The sooner I finish the sooner I can get out of here."

"You do know that you're not going anywhere, right? I mean, you're here until your six months are up." Renie didn't bother telling him that she didn't have that long, but she'd bet anything that he knew. "What have you found out about the accounts? Can you tell me why we're all losing money on a weekly basis?"

She didn't know this man. Nor, as with most people, did she trust him. But she handed him her notes, knowing that he'd no more be able to read them than if she'd written them in Spanish or some other language.

He studied them, and when he seemed to be reading them over, Renie went back to work. There was something there, something just on the edge of this that she could almost figure out. Bringing up the next page of numbers, she started to read them over when a number, the amount of it, touched something deep within her.

"What bank are these accounts with?" When he didn't answer her, she looked up. Not only was the man gone, but it looked as if the store was closing up as well. When Renie looked at the time in the lower right side of her computer, she was surprised to see it was well after seven o'clock.

Judith came toward her with a brown bag with the logo of the shop on it. "I'm going to take you to the apartment now if you're ready. You really get into your work, don't you?"

"It's what I'm supposed to be doing for you." If Judith had a comment, she didn't say it aloud. "Are you going to lock me in nightly? Is that how you're going to keep me here?"

Judith stopped on the stairs they were going up and Renie took a few steps back. There was fury there and Renie was afraid. When Judith put out her hand, Renie flinched from it as if she'd been struck, something that happened to her a lot.

"Who did this to you?" Renie looked where Judith had and pulled her sleeve back down over the large wound. "Did they hurt you in the jail, Renie? Did someone there do this to you?"

"I don't know what you're talking about." When she searched this time, Renie closed her out. "Don't. I don't need you trying to take care of me like a baby. I'm hurt but I'm sure that what's coming for me will be plenty worse."

"I heard about what happened to you. No one should...do you see her? Your mother? Do you know where she is?" Renie said nothing but Judith seemed to understand. "I guess that the two of you don't talk much, do you?"

They went up the stairs after a few more seconds. Renie felt like she'd been run over. Not just from fighting the woman to stay out of her thoughts, but she really was drained from everything that had happened over the last two weeks. As she was shown around the beautiful place, Renie asked what was going to be expected of her if she stayed there.

"Nothing but the work you were contracted to do. I need to know what is happening with my books. Something is always coming up missing. And there are other accounts, too, that are missing money...I don't know how to explain it." Renie had an idea but said nothing just now. "Anyway. If you want to work up here instead of down in the dining room, I'm okay with that. But don't be surprised if we bring you up meals. I think you'd forget to eat if we didn't."

After Judith left her, Renie walked around the spacious rooms again. The bedroom was huge, and fully furnished. The kitchen was complete with a small dinette table and two chairs, as well as all the things that she'd need, such as a coffee pot and a tea maker. The cabinets were full too. As she pulled down a cup with a small tin of teas, she thought of living there. It wouldn't be that bad if she could work up there all the time and not be bothered. Going to the living room area with her hot tea, Renie thought of her last conversation with her mother, Penny.

She'd gone to her house, the one that Renie had bought and paid for when she'd gotten her first million dollar contract. After sitting in the living room for over an hour and being ignored, her mother finally spoke to her. It wasn't really surprising that she didn't care for her, but Renie was hurt by her words all the same.

"I've no use for you any longer." Renie looked around the house, at the things in it that she'd paid for when her mother had money too. Not as much as Renie did, but she'd had it. She'd wanted to tell her mom that she'd gotten a better job, one that would pay her very well. That had gone over like it usually did. Nothing. "I want you to go away. You can send me money every month. It's the least you can do for how I had to be raped for you to be here. But I should tell you that you're dead to me now. You have been for a long time."

"I see. My money is good enough, just not me. Why have you always hated me? Is it because I've done something to you? It can't be just the rape. You do know that I had nothing to do with that, right?" Her mother just stared right through her. "Penny, why do you hate me?"

"I sold you to him." Renie asked her who she was talking about. "That demon. I called to him one night when you were a baby still screaming in your bed and I told him to take you away. He said he would later."

"Later?" Her mother looked at her then, and Renie could see the insanity. It had always been there, but it was more visible now. "What are you talking about? What demon? You mean a drug dealer?"

"No. A fucking demon. Why is it you expect me to listen to you go on about shit I do not care about when you won't fucking give me the same curtesy? A fucking demon came here and I told him he could have you, but I wanted to live forever." Renie wanted to tell her she was nuts, but she thought perhaps this time her mom might have been telling her the truth. "He said I could live forever and once you turned twenty-five, something about you being made just for him and that you'd be the payment. And you will go with him, Reyna. I've suffered a great deal because of you. You owe me this."

Renie had sat there while Penny told her what he'd said to her. That Renie would be his, his bed partner, until such time he grew bored with her. Then he would let his minions have her. She would be in hell for the rest of her days. Her mother had taken great pleasure in telling her this, Renie could see.

"Why? Why did you tell him you'd give me to him? Why didn't you just put me up for adoption if you didn't want me? I don't understand why you'd do this to me after I've done all this for you." Her mother just shrugged. "You just gave away your child because you had no more use for me? Or was it because of something else? What was it, Mother? What made you give me to a fucking demon?"

"Because I hate you and everything about you."

That had been about two years ago. Since then she'd seen her mother once more, and it had not gone any better than the last time. But this time she'd come away with the contract between her and this demon. Her mother didn't know that of course, but Renie had it. And she'd not found a single thing in it that would let her out of her mother's promise except one thing. And that was fucking going to never happen, even if she didn't fully understand it.

Chapter 2

Arryn watched the children playing in the yard. He was there with his own charge, but he watched him with a heavy heart. The child would not see his next birthday and everyone knew it. Boss had even been kind enough to tell him the date of the young man's death. It would be the day after tomorrow. He would simply go to sleep and never wake.

"He is having fun, it seems." Arryn didn't look at Michael when he spoke, but nodded. "I have come to tell you that when he comes to us, Boss would like for you to be with him until he is settled. It will only be for an hour or two, but he fears he will be very upset about things."

"I'll stay, but I don't think you're going to have any problems. He is ready, I think. I've been…preparing him." Michael thanked him. "I hate when children die. I understand that it has to be, and he does suffer so much daily, but I do not have to like it."

"None of us do." They both looked on as the boy's mother came to wheel him closer to the swings. He was no longer able to sit in them, his body was so sore and weak. But he did enjoy watching the others play. "There is someone I'd like for you to see. Not…she is most unusual, and Boss would like for you to spend her remaining days with her."

"I can't. I know that this is an assignment that you need me to do, but I can't watch another child die. Not right now." Michael told him she wasn't a child but a full grown woman. "Then have her own protector take care of her. I just can't."

"She's your other half, Arryn. I was to tell you that before you meet her. But she has...Boss has missed something with her and she will only live for a few more months before she will be taken away." Arryn looked at him. "Her soul belongs to another."

"I don't understand what you mean." Michael nodded again and Arryn continued. "You mean she's meant for the underworld and you want me...he picked her for my wife, and then she's to be taken from me? I just...why would you do that to me?"

"I have told you, there was a mistake." Arryn said nothing but watched his young charge. "There was no mention of her name on the charts. We know, it's the way we do things when someone has gone to the other side. But this was done without her knowledge. Without any of our knowledge. Her mother did this. Sold her to the demon for the chance to live forever."

Arryn looked at Michael before speaking. "That's not possible. Why would a mother sell her child to a demon? You must have it wrong."

"Nay, I do not. Only if that could make it right. But in a few short months she will go and we will all feel her loss." Arryn would not be one of them. He would not do this, he told Michael. "You will refuse this?"

"I must. I know that...I have seen the others with their mates. Even after such a short time, they are besotted with them to the point of silliness. I cannot…I would suffer greatly should this come to pass, and I think you cruel for asking me to do this. Nay, Michael, I fear neither my heart nor my mind could take this willingly."

"I thought as much." Michael stood up and Arryn stared at him, almost waiting for him to tell him he had to do it. Arryn even had himself prepared for such a fight, because fight he would. "I will inform Boss. I would not be able to do this either, Arryn. Perhaps…well, it matters little now. Good day to you."

After Michael left him, Arryn sat there for a long time. He watched his charge, and saw how Jim suffered greatly when another child made cruel remarks to him. Arryn went to him then and told him that others did not understand him, could never understand him, and that he was a brave boy for not lashing back at the child. As they traveled home Arryn told him over and over what a brave and strong boy he was, and told him to cherish the fun he'd had with his mother.

Late that night, with the child sleeping with his monitors on and the nurse dozing lightly in the chair next his bed, Arryn thought about the young woman. Who could do this to their child, sell them to something like a demon?

"I know that you're there." Arryn sat up on his perch and waited for Jim to say more. "I know that you watch over me all the time and keep me safe."

"It is my job." It was the first time he'd ever spoken to a charge directly. Arryn let him see him too. "You should be resting. Tomorrow you and your mother are going to the pool, if I remember correctly."

"It will be my last outing with her." Arryn said nothing. It was true, but he didn't tell him that. "I'm very tired; you know that, don't you? My body is hurting more and more each day. And I know…I've figured out that it won't be long now. She thinks that I can't hear her."

Arryn had heard his mother as well. She cried nightly for her child, and there was no one there to help her with her grief. Her mate—husband—had left her a few years ago when it was apparent that young Jim was not going to get any better.

"She will miss you greatly, but you will no longer suffer as you are now." Jim nodded and lay there, so very still. "Should you like to know when? I am not supposed to tell you this, but it might help you when you have your outing to help her."

"She needs this. Not to know that I'm going to be gone soon, but this outing with her. She…Mom will hurt so much when I'm gone. I don't want her to cry, but I know that she will." Arryn told him it was because she loved him with all her heart. "If I could…do you think it possible that I could see her when I'm gone? You know, visit her to make sure she's going to be okay?"

"It would not be good for either of you should you do that. She will…a mother will know that her child is with her, and it will be harder for her to…not forget you, but to have the pain of your passing lessen a little more each day. And you will need to adjust to your life too. Seeing your mother so much would only hurt you longer and longer until you both are suffering more than you do now." Jim nodded and wiped at the tears. "Do not cry for her, Jim. She will suffer, yes, but she will not leave you when the time comes. You will not be alone when you pass."

"Did you love her?" The question startled him and he asked him what he meant. "Whoever you miss when…when one of us dies. You said this was your job. So I'm betting that there was someone that died that you miss a lot. Did you love her?"

Arryn had not thought of her in many years…not fully anyway. She was always a part of him, but he never…. "Yes. I loved her. Very much. But not in the way that a man loves a woman. She was…her kindness touched me in ways that no one had before or since."

"I bet she was a good mom too. Mine is the best." Jim closed his eyes and Arryn realized what this might be costing him. He told him he must rest, but Jim shook his head. "I will rest soon enough. I just want to…I remember when my dad lived here and he would try to get me to play ball. I wanted to play with him so bad, but I just couldn't do it. It hurt."

"I was there." Jim nodded and his smile grew. "Your mother helped you. She said that she'd hold the bat for you and you'd hit it. Do you remember what she said to you when you hit the ball?"

"She said it was a grand slam." Jim looked at him. "You were always there for me. I remember…you spoke to me today too. I thank you for that. What's your name?"

"Arryn. They call me Arryn the Avenger. I am that bad." Jim laughed then coughed hard. The nurse woke and helped him to sit up a bit, but his mom came in and took over. When she laid in the bed with Jim, Jim spoke as if they were still alone.

"Don't leave me alone." He told him he would not and his mother told him the same. "I love you."

"I love you as well." His mother cried that night, hard but quietly. Arryn's heart broke as well as he watched her hold her son like he was her world. He supposed that he was. He watched over them both until the sun came up.

And then he watched the little man take his last breath, a day sooner than he'd been told.

Jim stayed with his mom while she sobbed at his passing, and asked to stay with her until the doctor came...he didn't want to leave her alone just yet. Holding Arryn's hand, he told his mom over and over how much he loved her, how much better he felt. When the police came with the ambulance, Arryn told him it was time. As Jim's body was carried away, Arryn took his charge with him. They were seated, waiting for the word that he could pass through, when Jim looked up at him.

"You have to find love, Arryn the Avenger. If you don't, then...then everything will have been for nothing. You have to try." Arryn held Jim's hand and told him he'd try. "No. You can't try. You have to do it. Do it for me. Even if it's just for a minute, you have to find someone to love you. So...well, I guess you don't die, but she will. Don't let her die all by herself."

Arryn sat in the waiting room for what seemed like only minutes, thinking about what he'd said to him. Jim had...someone had put him up to it, he first thought. Then he realized that no one would do that, least of all Michael or Boss. But he didn't want to find love. Not with this woman, not when she belonged to another. Going to his rooms, Arryn sat on his bed thinking. He just could not do it.

~~~

Kala sat as still as she could. Something was wrong and she was afraid that it was trouble for her babies. She had three weeks to go and she wasn't as ready for them as she'd hoped she would be by now. Of course, she would have been had someone not confined her to bed and hired people around the clock to make sure she stayed there.

When the pain in her back took her breath away again, she looked up at Dusty.

Almost as if she knew that she was looking at her, Dusty looked up from her drawing. It was another ad campaign and Kala had been throwing out ideas since she'd come to see her. But the look on her face must have alarmed Dusty, because she stood up, dropping everything to the floor as she did.

"What is it? The babies? You?" Kala nodded. "I don't want to freak you out or nothing, but that fucking didn't help me."

"Yes, the babies and me. Does that help?" Dusty nodded, then shook her head. "And how do you suppose that is helpful?"

Dusty laughed. "Yeah, not so much. Who should I call for you? Riss? He'll be no help if this is the real deal. The last time we thought this was it, I thought we were going to have to sedate him instead of you."

"I think we should call the doc—" Her water broke. She felt it as it flooded the bed and her legs. "This is the real deal. Get them all."

The room was suddenly not just filled with people, but they were on the ceiling as well. Wings as wide as them were spread out as they hovered over her and the bed. The only one that seemed to be calm was Boss, and He told them all to leave. In the next heartbeat, they were alone save Dusty and Riss.

"We're ready for this if you are." Kala told Him she had been ready for weeks. "So you have. So you have. We have a very good doctor coming now. I have handpicked him myself. Riss, are you going to faint again?"

"No. I don't...is this really it? We're having our babies?" Kala nodded at her husband and he looked a little faint. "I'm ready. I think."

"Well, I certainly hope so. Or do you want me to try to put them back again? I'm still working on that, should you like to know." Riss covered his cock and backed from her. Kala looked at Boss, who was laughing loudly. "This is not funny. I'm...why am I not in pain?"

"You just hold my hand and we'll not have any of that. You're too precious to me to let you suffer for the birth of our first baby protectors." Kala nodded and looked at the man dressed in all white. It was blinding in its purity and she smiled, thinking of angels made in snow. When His wings spread out behind Him, Kala felt as if everything was going to be just fine. And when Riss kissed her cheek, Kala told him she loved him.

There was a little pain, mostly pressure she thought, but when the doctor told her to push, Kala wasn't sure what to do. Her mind, like her body, seemed to not belong to her. Then she saw Arryn. He was standing behind the doctor and she could tell that something had happened.

"Arryn?" He nodded but said nothing. "Come here. Tell me what happened. Did Jim pass away?"

"You can talk to him later, my dear. Things are progressing quickly now." Kala wanted to tell him to leave her alone, she'd talk to who she wanted to, when she felt an enormous weight being lifted from her. Then her first son was laid upon her chest.

The rest was a blur. She knew that they were healthy and that someone was caring for them, but for the life of her, all Kala could focus on was Riss. His face was right in front of her, telling her to breathe when she was ready to pass out, or to tell her she was doing fine. She didn't think she was, but soon she was told to close her eyes. And she did.

The room was quiet when she woke. Kala reached out into the room and knew that Boss was there as well as Riss. But the man standing in front of the dark window was who she wanted to talk to most of all. Calling out for Arryn to come to her, she wasn't surprised when he moved silently across the room.

"They are beautiful. I've seen them all. Riss would not allow any of us to touch them until you did, but we did peek in on them several times. You did a wonderful job." She asked him if Riss had fainted. "No. I was surprised by that myself. He was strong and sturdy. Do you have names picked out yet?"

"Yes." He nodded and she saw the sadness again. "Did Jim pass away today? I'm sorry if he did."

"He died in the arms of his mother, as it should have been." Kala nodded, but before she could ask him anything else, he continued. "He knew I was there. He spoke to me with his last breaths. Told me that I should find love and enjoy it."

"And you should." He nodded. "She's here. You were told that she's here. Did you meet her yet?"

"No." He looked away and she knew that he was hurting. "There won't be much time for us. I don't want to hurt any more, Kala. I have suffered enough."

Kala wanted to feel sorry for him, but the more she lay there thinking of what he'd just said, the more pissed she became. So she did what she wanted and slapped him in the back of the head.

"What is wrong with you? You don't want to suffer? Well, poor Arryn the Whiney-Ass is going to be suffering; let us stop the presses and print him a get well card. We just can't have you suffer, now can we?" He started to speak again but she cut him off. "Oh, no you don't. You don't get to sit here and tell me how you're the one that is going to lose out. How your one true love is going to leave you soon after you've found her because of something that she had no control over. Poor, poor you. You mother fucking dick head."

"Why are you mad at me?" He stood up then, and Kala was vaguely aware that everyone in the room was awake and staring at them. "You have no idea what it's like to have someone you've come to love die. Life after life, century after century."

"No, I don't, thank goodness. But you will never know the love of someone that was meant for you. No, you'd rather sit here and bemoan the fact that you're going to be hurt when she dies. When she's taken to hell, I mean. Do you suppose the demon that has her...do you think he'll care that she's young and never been loved?" He said nothing but she didn't care. "What do you suppose is going to happen to her once she's there, Arryn? Do you think she'll get to have a nice room of her own? That she'll be treated with the utmost respect and care? Or do you think she'll be raped daily, if not hourly? Used as a sex slave while others—men who don't care one fig about her while they do it—watch her suffer. But you just can't think of that. Your suffering will be so much worse, won't it? What will you do? Pout in your room with the controlled temperatures and lovely views, while someone fixes you meals and comes by and talks to you on occasion to see if you're still suffering?"

"You're not being fair. This was not of my making." Kala stood up and stared at Arryn when he spoke again. "You are looking at this as if I have any control over it. I would be forced into this in much the same way that you and Riss were forced into what you have."

The slap she gave him startled her as much as it did him, Kala thought. But when he put his hand on his cheek all she could think about was this woman. Instead of telling him what a fool he was, Kala got back into the bed.

"Go away, Arryn. Don't come back here for a while. I'm not sure…I just don't want to see you right now." Rolling to her side and with her back to him, she wiped at the tears. "And stay away from Renie, too. I'm not doing this so you'll go to her, but I genuinely want you to stay the hell away from her. She doesn't need an asshole like you during her last days on this earth."

She knew that he'd left her, but she no longer cared. He'd hurt her as surely as he'd stabbed her in the heart. To have brought up what she and Riss had as if it were a terrible thing…. When arms slid around her from behind, Kala let Riss hold her as she lay there crying. This was supposed to be a great day for them all, and now it was ruined.

Kala woke some time later. The room was brighter so she knew that she'd been asleep for a while. Riss was the only one in the room with her, and he was holding a blue bundle in his arms. Sitting up, she looked around the bed and noticed that there were three more little blue bundles laying on the bed with her. Picking one up, she smiled down at his lovely face. The shifting of the bed had her looking at Riss when he sat down beside her.

"You did a wonderful job bringing them into the world. And they are simply perfect. I was thinking that we should have Boss model every child after these four. What do you think?" Kala laughed at him and he smiled.

"You're much more beautiful now than when I first met you."

"I love you too." They took the blankets off their sons and looked them over. Kala was thrilled to see that they each had all their toes and fingers, as well as the most amazingly tiny hands and feet that went with them. Their tiny little mouths were puckered up just so, and she wanted to kiss them all over their small bodies. When she touched her fingers to the first little nose, it crinkled up just as hers did.

"They have been asking after their names. Do we know which will be which?" Nodding, she looked at Riss, the man that made this all possible for her. "You look very teary. Is it the hormones again? Shall I get you some tea? It calms you like nothing else will."

"No. I'm fine. I was thinking of the way that I treated Arryn. I shouldn't have said those things to him." Riss sat up and pulled her and the baby that she held into his arms. "You're very sweet to hold me like this. Unless it's to keep me from hurting you when you tell me what a fool I was."

"I think you did what was correct. He needed to be told that he was...I think you called him a whiney-ass baby. No, that was not it, you called him Arryn the Whiney-Ass. Quite good, by the way. I thought perhaps that Boss was going to hurt Himself; He was trying His best not to laugh." Kala smiled, thinking of the big man trying not to laugh. She might have hurt Him and He knew it. "Arryn has gone to his world now. I don't believe he will be back for some time. You have shamed him well."

Nodding, she let Riss hold her until the babies stared to fuss. She had decided to breast feed them as best she could, but four of them was going to be too much. So while she fed two of them, Riss would have help feeding the other two. She talked to him while trying to figure out how to make it work.

"I was so pissed at him. He had no right to talk about his own pain when she was going to have so much more." Riss said nothing as he tried to get the baby to take the bottle. As soon as the babies at her breasts latched onto her nipples, she knew that she could do this. She also knew that she'd need help, but she wasn't going to fail these little men of hers.

"He will come around. Hopefully not too late. She does not have much...how did you get them to take to that so readily?" Kala told him she just squirted a little into their mouth and they wanted more. "I shall do that. As for Arryn, he will be all right. A little less whiney assed, I think, but he will come around."

It took them over two hours to get the babies fed and then changed. She knew that in a little while she was going to have to start over, but for now they were filled up and dry. The nurse that they'd hired came in to see if they needed anything, and a large tray of food was sent up for her and Riss. Boss came by later to ask them if they were all right and to hold one of the children. Kala fell asleep again and never heard Him leave.

Chapter 3

The computer printout was not matching up to what was in the bank. Renie knew that was why she'd been asked to go over it, but it wasn't the accounting program that was messing it up…it was something else, something that the bank was doing. Or someone at the bank. When the pounding at the door nearly brought her up out of the chair, she glared at the door trying to get her heart back to normal speed. Whoever was on the other side had better have a damned good reason for scaring the shit out of her. But before she opened the door, she paused in front of it to feel the person on the other side.

She could feel his sorrow even before she looked to see who it was. When he pounded on the door again, she backed away from it to hide…not from him, but from his pain. Whatever had hurt him, she wanted no part of.

"I know that you're in there. They told me downstairs that you never leave this room." She backed all the way to the work table she'd been using. "I could come through the door and simply talk to you, but I would rather you let me in. Please. I will not harm you."

"You've no business with me." His pain was replaced with anger, and she felt her own shields come up when he reached out to her mind. "You want to hurt yourself, then by all means try to figure out what makes me tick. But you'll hurt more for your troubles than anything you might find out."

"Boss sent me. And if you don't know who He is, He's the man that bargained for your help at your hearing. He sent me here. Sort of." Renie didn't move but knew who he was talking about…the big man who had looked as if He'd had His heart ripped out. "May I please come in and talk to you? Judith and Dusty are ready to murder me. Not that they can, but they will harm me."

Renie went to the door and took off the chain. There wasn't a lock on it, but the chain had stopped most of the unwanted guests from just coming in. Even after telling them repeatedly that she liked to be alone, they still came by in droves. The man standing there looked like he could take them all on and have them for breakfast. When he looked at her, she felt as if she'd been turned inside out.

"What do you want?" She stood in front of the doorway to bar him from coming in, but he was either dense or didn't care what anyone wanted as long as it was his way. Barging in, he stomped into the room as if he owned it. Renie stood in the doorway and tried to think what to do with him. "I didn't say you could come in. In fact, I would rather that you didn't. I'm busy."

"You've been up here for three days. And nights. What could you possibly be doing that requires you to stay indoors?" Renie crossed her arms over her chest and glared at him. "You're very tiny, aren't you? I don't know why, but I expected you to be tall, like Kala. You're not much more than five ten or so."

"To most that would be more than tall enough. Not that it matters what you think about my height, but you're very tall. Perhaps that's why you think I'm so short." He nodded and she waited. She was very good at waiting people out. They usually tired of her not speaking to them, but she had a feeling this guy was very good at it too.

"I'd like to take you to dinner. There is a nice place just down the street that has a very good steak dinner that—"

"No." He looked confused, and she put her hand on the still open door and opened it wider. "Now if you don't mind, I have work to do. And in the event that no one has told you, I'm sort of on a timeframe here."

"Why?" She asked him what he meant. "Why are you going to just let him take you? Can't you think of anything to do to get him to change his mind?"

"I'm not sure I want to. And so you know, I'm pretty sure that when one makes a deal with the devil, he expects you to pay up." He shook his head. "Do you have some firsthand knowledge that others don't about him?"

"Sort of. But the deal wasn't made with the devil. He wouldn't have cared if you were a babe or not. Had he wanted you, he would have taken you. But not without your consent." Something in what he said triggered a memory, but it was gone before she could catch it. "It was made with a demon, not the devil. Do you know his name?"

"Hum, the last time he and I talked he told me. Now what was it…?" She looked up at him when he huffed. "What the hell do you care for? And how the hell would I know his name, even if I cared what it was?"

"I was only trying to help you." Renie nodded to the door again. "I can't leave you. I have to…it's my duty as your true love to stay here to give you comfort when you die."

Renie let his words soak in. There was no way he'd just said that to her, but the longer he stood there staring at her, the more she realized that he had indeed. It was his duty? To stay with her?

"I see. And this duty of yours, does it by chance include us having sex? Lots of it?" She saw him stiffen just before he told her he would if she wished. "Good. And this sex—because I want to make sure that we're on the same page—will this sex be beneficial to us both, or are you a fuck'em and leave them sort of man?"

"I've never had sex before. I think you should explain what you mean." What she wanted to do was pick up the nearest sharp thing and stab him in the eye with it. "You seem to be getting angry rather than sexually aroused. Is there something I can do to help you? I don't know what I can do, but I have seen others have sex and I could mimic them."

"Yes. You can get the hell out of here." The man started to speak but she cut him off. "You arrogant mother fucking prick. What gives you the right to come in here and tell me about your duty to me? And that you're to stay with me, like it is some kind of chore that you'd rather not do but are being forced into? Is that it? Someone is forcing you to come here?"

"She has guilted me into this. I don't think that it was her intention, but that is what I feel. She's very upset with me. And I love Kala like a sister, and it pains me when I have disappointed her in some way. I would like to make it up to her by doing what she thinks is best for you. She will be happy that you're not alone in your time of need, and I will not be in her bad graces." Renie told him to get out. "But we have not settled on anything. I should like to—"

"If you do not get out of here right this fucking minute I'm going to scream. And when I scream, strange and very violent things begin to happen. The last time I brought a building down on a few people. I'm pretty sure that as pissed as I am right now, I could easily bring down a city block." He stood there as if he wasn't going to go anywhere. Renie closed her eyes and reached out to him.

When he cried out she knew that she had hurt him. But right now hurting him was much better than what she really wanted to do to him. Willing him to the street beyond, she realized that she should have looked to see if there was any oncoming traffic when a car's tires screamed. *Serves him right if a car hit him.* But she went to check to make sure that he'd not been killed.

After he moved along the street, never looking up at the window where she was, Renie went to the kitchen and stared into the refrigerator. A woman clearing her throat had her putting up her hands in defense.

"I'm Lily. I have brought you something to drink." Renie could smell the sugar from where she was. Taking the tall glass, Renie drank it down and watched as it refilled itself without a pitcher. Drinking the second glass down, she stared at the woman.

"Thank you. Nice trick." Lily told her that she'd only brought the first glass, that Renie had filled it again. "I didn't know that I could do that, but I guess there is all kinds of shit going on that I don't know about. Like who are you, and what the fuck are you doing here?"

"Lily Anderson. I'm like the others. I know that you've not been introduced to us yet, but I'm here to show you. Boss thought it a good idea since your magic is coming on stronger now. Is it because of Arryn?" Renie told her she didn't know him. "The man that you sent to the streets. Very good job at that, by the way. I would have blasted him to the next realm. I've never known him to be so rude before."

"He wouldn't leave." Lily nodded. "You're not going to hang around now, are you? I have things to get done."

"You do. But I do want to explain what we are. Do you know what a protector is?" Renie shook her head and sat down on the lovely couch that had been with the living room. Lily sat opposite her. "We are a group of beings—immortal beings—that watch over humans from their first breath until their last. Then when that time comes, we take them to their destination, where they will stay forever."

"So you think you're an angel." Lily told her no, they were entirely different than her. "I'm sorry, but you're not really making any sense. Not that I really care, but you really should have a better story if you're going to tell one. Like mine. I'm going to be the playmate to a demon. Tonight I found out that it's not the devil himself, but I guess one of his lesser beings. And in being so, he will come for me when I turn twenty-five. Not long now."

"You readily believe in devils and demons and not angels?" Renie said nothing. "I have heard that you were lost to us. That your mother sold you to him and we did not find out until recently."

"Same here. And not that you'd understand, but I'd prefer that you didn't refer to Penny Sharp as my mother. She's the woman who brought me into this world, and because she thought that living forever was preferable to having me, she sold me for immortality. So she's going to be the one to take me out, too. Nice, huh?"

"I'm sorry." Renie waved her off. "I do have to tell you some things. And it will go easier if you believe me."

"Why? And that man, who was he besides some lunatic that thinks I should let him fuck me?" Lily said his name again and smiled. "And this Arryn person, he's sane? Like you?"

"I'm very sane, Reyna Lynn Sharp." Renie thought that there was a saying that everyone thought they were sane when in actuality they were not. "I would like to show you something."

When Lily stood up, Renie sat up straighter in her seat. She had no idea why this woman, of all the people she knew, had her trusting in what she said, but there was something very innocent about her. She was off her rocker, of course, but she trusted her. But when wings sprung out from behind her, spreading as wide as her couch, Renie stood up.

"Mother fuck." Lily didn't move when Renie walked toward her. As she stood there watching her, the snowy white wings moved and Lily was lifted from the floor. Renie started to reach out to touch the beautiful display, but pulled her hand back when it began to burn. "I'm not supposed to touch you."

"You may." Renie shook her head and looked down at her hand. There were blisters on it, and she tried to hide it from her when Lily grabbed her hand and held it out. "This is not to happen. You should not burn when one of us is...did this happen when Arryn was near you?"

"He wasn't. Near me, I mean. Do you think you could let go now? I'm on fire." Her fingers were actually burning, with small flames coming from them. As soon as Lily let her go, the fire went out but the pain was still there. Renie fell to her knees. "I'm going to be sick."

Before she could make her way to the bathroom several armed men were in her apartment...not armed

39

with guns, but swords and in armor of such beauty that she nearly stopped to stare at it. Ignoring them was nearly impossible when she had to dodge them to get to where she needed to be. Just as she got the door shut behind her to the bathroom, she puked. On her knees now, Renie emptied her belly five times before she felt as if she might not die right now.

A soft cloth was put on her forehead as Renie leaned on the now closed toilet. Not even bothering to look up, she thanked the person. When Arryn spoke she didn't even have the strength to tell him to get the hell away from her. She was spent.

"I am sorry that I hurt you." Renie didn't say anything. She really was that weak that she wanted him gone but did not have the energy to tell him to get out. "I should like to see if my touching you will burn you as well. I'll not hold you, only touch my finger to your flesh."

"Have all the fun you want. I don't have the strength to fight you right now." His fingers on her arm felt cool to the touch. When he wrapped his hand around her she moaned at how good it felt, and nearly sobbed when he pulled away. But he picked her up then and sat her on the counter. "I'd like to go to bed now. Why don't you come back tomorrow and you can insult me some more? Right now I'm not into it."

He didn't say anything but she felt herself being picked up again. When things moved by her quickly, Renie closed her eyes. It was making her sick again. Then the coolness of her bed was under her and she moaned again. Renie felt a cover being pulled over her and then she let sleep take her.

~~~

Arryn didn't want to leave her, but he needed to tell the others that he was staying with her. Even if he had to stay with her while she couldn't see him, he wasn't leaving her. He'd not only hurt her earlier, but he had been shamefully cruel to her. Boss and Michael were the other two in the room when he came out of her bedroom.

"Did you heal her?" Arryn expected Michael to be upset with him when he told him he had. "Good. She was in a great deal of pain, and Lily felt as if she might not heal quickly from the burns. You did not harm her, I take it?"

"I asked her permission to touch her before I did, and when it didn't blister her, I picked her up. She doesn't weight much, does she?" Boss shook his head when he and Michael looked at Him. "I've done her a great disservice. I should like to make it up to her."

"I think she will be hard to convince of that, but you may try." Boss looked at Michael, who nodded and left them. Boss asked Arryn to have a seat. "I heard what you said to her. What she said to you. You two are more violate than I had thought a couple could be."

"I was not...it was my fault. I should have taken better care with my words with her. And my anger." Boss nodded. "What can you tell me about her? I should like to know what I can do to make this easier on her."

He told him of her conception, of how her mother treated her, and of the magic that she had. "She has more, a great deal more, than you might have witnessed today. But I thought...I'm thinking that you're giving her strength when you are near her. I'm not sure...I honestly did not think it would appear for some time now. Not until the two of you were together."

"You mean sexually." Boss nodded and leaned back in His chair. "I have no wish to...sex is not something that came up when we were together earlier. She is most...I would say that she is very vocal in her displeasure with me."

Boss laughed. It was a hardy one and a sound that made Arryn smile despite the issues he was having right now. He thought that it had been a while since he'd heard it for any reason.

"Arryn, she is very displeased with you. Not that I blame her much. What were you thinking when you told her it was your duty to be here with her?" Arryn had no idea and said as much. "I would really try and take care of my words should you ever get the chance to talk to her again. As I have said, she is stronger now that you are near her."

"Can she be saved?" Boss said He was looking into it. "I have asked her what the demon's name is that holds her, but she either doesn't know or won't tell me. I think it could be both."

Boss nodded before speaking. "Should you find out, it would make things easier on us. I can have a talk with him, or if that fails maybe we can buy her more time. I know that it would hurt you more to spend time with her, but I would ask that you try to make it work."

Arryn said that he would and looked to the closed door to the room where she was. "Why did she burn so badly with Lily, and not with my touch? What is it that makes that happen?" He looked at Boss when there wasn't an answer. "I should really like to know, sire. She is my charge for now, and perhaps my lover soon."

"The demon is laying claim to her. It's all I can think of. Or a curse has been put upon her. Probably a little of both." Arryn asked how that was possible. It wasn't time yet. "No, but whoever he is, he has to know where she is and who she is with by now. It will be harder on him, I guess, to know that she's with my people now."

"I will give her all the comfort I can. And should we become lovers, it will be because she has said it was good and not because I have forced it upon her." Boss said He knew that. "I'm not sure about her or me, but I will not...I will try not to anger her again."

After Boss left him, Arryn wandered around the room. It was neat and clean with the exception of the table where she had her work spread out. He didn't touch it, not even to see what she was doing. He had his own way of doing things and was very upset when it was moved. He would have bet that she would know if he even touched the pencil that laid on her papers. He would.

When night came he moved to her room. As hard as he tried, there was no way he was going to fit into the tiny chair made for someone about half his size. And the couch, while it was bigger, wouldn't fit him either. Moving to the bed, he called himself all kinds of a fool as he took off his shirt and shoes. She would most assuredly kill him when she woke up.

As soon as she rolled into him, Arryn wrapped his arms around her. When he'd picked her up earlier he'd not just been surprised by how slight she was, but also just how tiny she was. He supposed she was tall for what humans were, and she did fit nicely under his chin, but he was almost afraid to break her. And that, to him, was funny.

"I've no knowledge of anyone holding me before. I have been hugged, but by other protectors. Male and female, as a matter of fact." Arryn had no idea why he was talking to her, he knew her to be sound asleep. "You feel good here. In fact, I think that this is the best I've felt in a long while. My job...it's not a job, I suppose, but something that I enjoy. But this last one, it was difficult for me."

"Don't hurt me." He started to tell her that he'd never do that to her again when she stiffened in his arms. "No. Don't hurt me. Please?"

"I shall not harm you. And I will not let others." When she sat up, nearly taking his head off when she did, he sat up as well. His wings were under him, but he knew that whatever she was seeing, in her dream or thoughts, he couldn't do a thing to it.

"I can't do what you want. I know you say that you'll give me back my life, but I just can't do that. I have no reason to do that. I'm ready for whatever bullshit you do to me." Arryn reached out to touch her, and as soon as he did, he saw what she was seeing. It was...it was as if he'd entered her dreams with her. Only he was sure this was not just a dream. "I don't care for them, but I won't do what you want."

"Then you will die." The demon in front of them was blurred. Arryn wasn't sure if he was to her or not, but figured that he was. "And you will suffer in ways you will not ever be able to get over. I will burn your flesh from you daily. Then I will fuck you until you think you have been turned inside out. And I will do this every day until you give me what I want."

"I won't give it to you. I won't do that. You can try and make me, but I'll fight you with my every breath." The demon moved closer to them then. He was in focus just a second, but it was long enough for Arryn.

"Then you will come to me or I will make you wish you had." Arryn wanted to ask her what she had to do, what it was the demon wanted, but he was gone before he could. And when she laid back down over him, her body trembling against his, Arryn reached for Boss.

I don't know who he is but I do know what he looks like. And he wants something from her in trade for her life. Boss asked what it was. *I don't know, but Renie does, and we'll figure this out.*

Kathi S. Barton

Chapter 4

Renie moved out of the bedroom and into her work area. She wanted to be pissed off because of the big hulking man in her bed, but when she'd woke with him wrapped around her, holding her, she thought she could get used to it. But then reality set in and she got up, keeping him in sleep until she was dressed and away.

The computer called to her. She wanted to sit down and figure out what she'd started yesterday, but food was needed. Not that she made anything elaborate, but a bowl of cereal was good enough. Problem was, there wasn't any in the cabinets. A noise behind her made her lift her hands in defense before she looked.

"It is I." Lowering her hands, she looked at Arryn. "I'm sorry I startled you, but I did say your name. Twice. What are you looking for?"

"Cereal. It's all I know how to cook this early." He moved into the kitchen and started pulling things from the refrigerator as well as the cabinets. "What are you doing now?"

"I'm making us something to eat. I'm hungry as well." She watched as a pan was put on the toy sized stove and then he put bacon in it. "I cook when I have time. It is something that I enjoy a great deal. I guess you do not."

"Not unless I don't have a phone to order something. It's expensive, but I get by." He nodded and she sat down when he poured her a glass of orange juice. "I don't want you to get into the habit of getting into bed with me. It's not…you're not welcome there."

"I slept soundly. Better than I have in a long while. Your bed is too short, but it was nice having you curl up to me." She felt her face heat up when she thought of just how curled around him she'd been. "You slept well then?"

"I guess. As good as I usually do." She thought about the conversation she'd had with her tormentor. "What are your plans for today besides leaving me alone?"

"I have no plans other than to protect you." She tried to think of a good reason he didn't need to protect her, but she couldn't think of any. To be honest, she was terrified of dying and ending up in hell. The person, the thing that came to her in her dreams was— "Would you like to tell me about it?"

It was on the tip of her tongue to tell him to leave her alone. But his voice had been soft, sort of comforting. Instead of telling him what she did everyone, Renie looked away and drew in a deep breath before beginning.

"This thing…person…I'm not sure, but she wants something from me. For me to do this thing for her…sometimes him…anyway, they want me to do something for them. I've already told them no, but they think that I will before this is over." Arryn asked her what it was. "It doesn't matter. Not really. I don't trust that they'll come through in the end, and whatever it is that they need from me will just be one more thing in a long line of fuck-ups that I'll have to think about."

"If you tell me who it is, perhaps we can have a talk with them." Arryn looked so earnest that she wanted to give him what he wanted, but she stood up instead and moved to the computer. "We have some really good connections, Reyna. Maybe we can help you in ways you've never thought of."

"I'm fine, Arryn. Trust me when I tell you, I was more than likely going to end up there as a result of my lifestyle anyway." She moved to the long table that she'd been using as a desk. "Let me know when you're ready to go; I'll have to lock up behind you."

Renie knew that she'd hurt him. It was her intention to do just that, because she knew as surely as she was sitting there that he'd be hurt, too, when this went down. Her cell phone ringing startled her and she nearly didn't answer it. There was only one person who had her number and she wasn't speaking to her. But she answered it in the end, thinking that maybe she'd had a change of heart. *And donkeys can fly*, Renie thought with a grin.

"Penny. What is it you want now? And if its money, forget it. I'm not *lending* you any anymore." Penny huffed at her but said nothing. "What is it? I'm working."

"It's not like you can take it with you. What do you have, two weeks, three? Just give it to me now. And then I won't have to wait until you're dead to get it. I have expenses. And this living a long time, it's going to continue to cost me." Arryn came to stand behind her and she let him listen. Why did she care if he knew about the woman who had given her over to hell? Penny continued on as if she had a right to everything else that Renie owned. "You shouldn't have stolen from me either. You bring that paper back to me right now or so help me, I'm going to tell him to take you now instead of whatever time you have left. You've been very ungrateful up until now, and I've had enough of it."

"I've been ungrateful? How do you figure that works? I've given you more than anyone could give a person. My life. Then there is the house, the car. I've paid off all your credit cards twice over." Penny huffed at her. "As for me stealing from you? Get real. That should be mine anyway, since I'm the one that you put out there so you could live for fucking ever."

Arryn didn't listen in on the call. His mouth moved along her throat almost like he was forging a trail to someplace better. When he cupped her breasts, lifting them up as he sucked at her throat, Renie saw stars. Penny yelling at her was distracting, and she pulled the phone to her mouth again.

"I'm busy. And I'm not giving you any money. Not now and not after I'm dead." Closing the connection, Renie leaned back in the chair. Arryn had pulled her shirt up now and her bra was lifted out of the way for his hands. Christ, his hands were warm.

"I'd very much like to taste you." Nodding, she moaned when he tugged at her nipple. "You're very responsive. And I love the way that your heavy flesh fills my hands. I want to take them into my mouth and nibble on the hard tips while my cock fills more."

"Is this your duty to me?" He growled low as his mouth moved down her chest. When he took her breast into his mouth, opening his mouth wide and sucking hard, she curled her fingers tightly into his hair and held him there. Then his hands slid down between her legs and rubbed along her pussy. "You're going to make me come if you keep this up. I'm very close right now."

"I should very much like to be inside of you when you do. Feel you tighten around me. I've thought of this since last night, when you curled your body around mine. What it would feel like to have you naked with me." The chair she was in was pulled back and he was on his knees in front of her. "Lift your bottom. I want to disrobe you so that I might see all of you."

Her pants and shoes came off all in one fluid moment. When he reached for her panties, Renie was almost embarrassed for him to see how wet she was. But when he pulled them off and took them to his nose, Renie almost came. As soon as he pulled her to the edge of the chair and spread her legs wide, Renie thought about what they were about to do…or what he was about to do.

"We could go to the bedroom. There's more room in there." He told her for now he was pleased. "Yeah, well, I'm going to be pleased here very soon. Don't you want to go in there?"

Arryn looked up at her and she felt her pussy gush again. Lust, need, and something she had no name for were there on his face for her to see. He leaned down to her pussy slowly, watching her as he did. When he touched his tongue to her curls, she held onto the sides of the chair tightly, knowing that when he touched her she was going to come apart.

"You're very wet. I can smell you as well." Nodding, she watched him, his movements so slow that she wanted to scream at him to touch her. "When I taste you, can I suck this tiny morsel into my mouth? Would you like that?"

"Yes." Nodding, he slid his hand up her thighs then between her open legs. Just shy of touching her, he massaged her muscles hard, then softly. "Please, your teasing me is driving me insane."

"I think I like you like this. Begging me to complete you. It will complete you...you know that, don't you?" Nodding again, she nearly cried out when he touched her clit with the barest of touches with his finger. "Here. Here is where I'd like to suckle you. Along with your nipples again. I so enjoyed the way your heart began to pound and the way that they seemed to swell for me."

"Arryn, take me. Please, just take me." Nodding, he finally lowered his head. When he lifted her up by her ass, she screamed when he put his mouth over her and sucked on her clit. And when he slid his tongue deep inside of her, she cried out again when a climax ripped around her. The third and then the fourth time she came, it was as if her entire life was meant for this one moment in time.

~~~

Arryn didn't know what he was doing, but every time she cried out, he would try something more. It was a test of her, seeing where he could bring her the most pleasure before he took his own. And he thought that watching her enjoyment was much better than his own release would ever be.

Her begging had him smiling. Arryn, of course, had heard women beg before. One did not work as a protector for all these decades without hearing or even seeing sex on occasion. But hearing her say those words to him, to have her beg him to stop, then for more, was making him ache in ways he'd never felt before. He reached down to free his cock before it hurt him more. The relief was profound, and he cupped himself to his body.

When her fingers jerked his head up, he looked at her. She was pink, her nipples were hard peaks, and her breathing was making him want to go back to what he was doing. He stood up when she told him, and stood back when she gave him a small push. But when she took his cock into her mouth, Arryn cried out. Nothing could have prepared him for the feeling of her hot mouth on him.

It wasn't just hot, but it was the wet feeling of it too. The way her tongue curled around his tip before she licked along his shaft. Every time she would swallow him down past the tightness of her throat, he felt as if he were being pulled in several directions at once, brought to the edge of a great cavern only to be pushed back again and again.

Curling his hand into her hair, he meant only to pull her back, to beg her to let him release on her, something to take care of the way he felt right now. But when she let go of his cock, a tiny pop emanating from her mouth when she did, all he could think about was sliding into her.

"I wish to take you. Now." Nodding, she stood up, still holding his cock in her hand. Then she leaned in and took his nipple, never a thing he had thought about, into her mouth, and he held her to him when she suckled at him as he'd done her. "Please, I am needy. I need to release."

"You will." As she moved away from him, he had no choice but to follow. Even had she not had her hand around his cock, he thought perhaps he'd go with her anywhere, at any time. But when she let him go and sat up on the counter, he had no idea where to go next. "Come here. You should fit me here. Your cock will be right at my pussy."

Almost leaping forward, he saw that she was right. Her womanhood was level with his throbbing cock.

Moving slowly into her, his tip was leaking so much that he was sure that it was going to disgust her, but when he pulled back she ran her fingers over the heavy cream and took it to her mouth.

"You like that taste? The taste of me in your mouth?" At her nod, she was touching him again, but this time it was to guide his cock into her sheath. "Slowly please. I'd like to enjoy this."

"Oh, we will. Very much so." He moved forward more, his cock buried inside of her. Arryn put his hands on the counter and then her hips. Pulling her to the edge, he slammed forward when she wrapped her feet around his hips, her legs pulling him in.

Arryn couldn't move. He wasn't even sure that he wanted to. Her sheath, the womanly part of her that he had filled, was stretching around him, pulling him deeper within her heat. And when she moved, her hips just lifting a little off the counter, Arryn felt his eyes roll to the back of his head and stay there.

It wasn't until Reyna leaned back, her breasts there for him like a feast, that he knew the real meaning of the word hunger. She was his, his mind screamed at him. His. Arryn leaned in and took just a tip into his mouth and bit down just as his hips moved on their own, filling her, then coming out to the tip again only to move deeper into her. Arryn looked down at his cock.

It was wet, covered with her juices as it slid in and out of her. Each time he moved she moaned, every time he filled her, she cried out, and her fingers at his shoulders dug deeper into his muscle as he pounded her. And when she screamed again, this time her body stiffened and bowed up, and Arryn felt his own release take him.

The stars behind his eyes seemed to explode into bright lights before fading out. His vision blurred and his body seemed to be perched just on the edge again before he fell over into a deep, wondrous cavern. Twice he felt himself empty into her, twice more she cried out his name, holding him to her even as his body continued to take her.

When she went limp in his arms, he held her. Arryn looked down at her, her body spent because of him, and he wanted to call everyone and tell them that he had a wife. But he gathered her into his arms and took her to the bedroom and the tiny bed that they had shared last evening.

Laying her on the bed, he stood back. She was bruised already from his strength. Leaning down to her tender flesh, he licked the wounds and was glad to see that they had disappeared. He hated that he'd hurt her, even in this way, but he was also feeling very good about what they had done. He wanted to check his own body for such markings and knew that were there any, he'd wear them like a badge for as long as they lasted. Dressing himself in things that he pulled to him with magic, he stared down at the things that had come to him to wear and wondered why he had thought of these things.

Never in his life had he wore anything that wasn't dressy. Some of the newer protectors, some as young as three or four hundred years old, had often teased him about his dress, but it was what he wore, what he was used to. But these pants — jeans, he thought them called — felt good on him. Tighter than what he normally wore, they were something that he could get used to. The shirt, a plain tee shirt much like the one he'd taken off Reyna, was made of the softest cotton, and he loved the texture of it as well.

Not bothering with shoes, he made his way to the kitchen again. He'd put the breakfast he'd been preparing on hold when he heard the distress in her voice. Arryn knew that it was her mother…Penny…but there was little he could have done to prevent the woman from calling her child. But when Reyna moved in the chair, her hair exposing her long neck, all he could think of was licking it. And once he'd done that, tasting it was next. He had had whole meals that would not have satisfied him as much as the tiny taste of her had. The way her skin felt in his hands and how her noises, the way she hummed and moaned, had sounded like the greatest music he'd ever heard. Then he thought of why he'd gone to her.

The call had upset her, very much so. As Arryn started to cook the potatoes that he'd found in the bottom of the cooking table, he wondered at the other woman's demands. Money. He knew that it was necessary to humans to live, but Penny Sharp was an immortal. What did she think she was going to do after her daughter was gone? There would be no one for her to take from. And that was another thing that had bothered him about the call. She had said that Reyna had stolen from her. What could the woman have that Reyna would take?

As soon as he heard the shower starting he moved into the bedroom. The bed was made, he noticed, and she'd picked up the few things that he'd left in the room when he'd gotten up. Nothing was out of place, but he felt there was something off about the room. When he couldn't see it he moved into the bathroom to see Reyna.

She was crying, and hard. As he moved to take her into his arms, she turned to him and told him to stop. He stopped, but it didn't lessen his concern for her. When she turned off the water and reached for a towel, he leaned against the counter.

"We shouldn't have done that." He asked her why not. "Because we're not going to have a relationship. I'm not going to be here long enough for anything like that. I'm sure that you remember what I told you. That I'm going to go to hell soon. That I'm going to be the sexual partner of a demon."

"We already have a relationship, and I'll take what I can get from you. But I will not give up so easily, and I can't believe that you have." She huffed at him and told him to get out so she could finish up. "I've seen every inch of you. I'd like nothing more than to taste you as well, but for now, I think we must talk. Why do you think that we cannot have a relationship?"

"I'm not going to be here very much longer. Why do I have to keep telling you that? Don't you listen? I'm not going to be around." He nodded and she huffed again. Arryn smiled at the sound and she glared at him. "This is not funny, damn it. I'm going to be taken to hell, and I don't want to have you hanging around here when he comes for me."

Standing up, he jerked her naked body to his. His cock thickened immediately and he put his arm around her waist and brought her up so that he could kiss her. She tasted of mint and something else. When he sat her back down on her feet, he held her steady until she was no longer swaying. Backing from her, he stared at her before speaking again.

"As I said, I will take what I can have with you. And if that means being here until you no longer need me, then I will. But I will not give you up to anyone without a fight. You belong to me." He handed her the small stack of clothing that was laying on the counter next to him. "I have breakfast nearly finished for when you are dressed; though now that I think on it, having you naked so that I might touch you and taste you when I please does sound very nice." She stared at him before he reached over and closed her mouth.

Arryn felt both bad for what he'd done to her and very good. Perhaps she needed to be brought out of the thoughts of her going to hell and to see what was all around her. He was going to work on that as soon as he could get her out of the apartment. If he could get her out. She seemed to enjoy working at the computer a great deal.

Arryn nearly laughed out loud when she came out of the bedroom. Instead of the pants and shirt she'd had to put on, she was now dressed in a thick sweat shirt and heavy pants that were sizes too big for her. He didn't comment on her apparel, but he did wonder about it. Handing her a filled plate and pushing her in the direction of the kitchen table, he took his own meal with him, as well as a gallon of juice and two glasses.

"I was thinking that I could take you to the exhibit that is in town. Lily and Kala have been working on this project to bring more culture into this part of the state for weeks now. And now that the babies have made an appearance, there will be more promise for celebration." Reyna nodded but he could tell she wasn't really paying attention. "She nor Riss has told us the names of the children as yet, but we have an idea that Boss knows. He is aware of everything."

"I have to finish this work. It's part of my sentencing." Arryn had forgotten about that and asked her how it was coming. "I'm not sure. There is something missing and I can't connect the dots to it yet."

Arryn didn't know what that meant but nodded to her. "Perhaps if you told me what you were doing, I could be a new set of eyes for you."

"There is money missing each month. Not a set amount that I can see, but a lot of it. Do you...I was going to ask Judith if she had other accounts too. Maybe the bank is moving the money in and out of the other accounts to give her a cushion." Arryn nodded. She smiled at him and he smiled back. "You have no idea what I'm talking about, do you?"

"Missing money I understand. Accounts, yes, I get that as well. But not the sofa part." She frowned, then laughed. "There is no sofa, is there?"

"No. Cushion, as in something to fall back on in an emergency. Like...." She looked around the room. "Like how someone filled these pantries. They had no idea what I would eat or not eat, so they filled it with lots of things. A cushion for me to use until I could go and buy what I want. Money is the same. They might be moving it around in the account to make sure that she never runs out. A fall back."

He understood it now and asked her again to tell him what she was doing. "So you think that the bank has taken it upon themselves to make her a cushion? But doesn't she have a great deal of money in her accounts? It was my understanding that all of us have more than enough to have the entire sofa I was asking you about."

"I don't know. She does have a lot of money, in all the accounts. So do the other three firms I'm looking into. But if this was common practice for the bank, I think Judith would have told me. But we're talking a lot of money. And while there is a lot in these accounts, I can't imagine that the bank would fuck with it. Not to mention, Judith doesn't strike me as a lax person when it comes to her money. Or her business's. I guess that's why she called me in." He said nothing, not really sure what he could say. "I'm thinking that the person or persons doing this think that with the amount of money she has in the accounts, she'd not notice that some of it was missing. I don't think, like I said, that Judith is the type of person to let something like this slide by."

Arryn finished his breakfast while she told him what she'd found. He tried to get Reyna to eat more than just the few bites that she did, but she was drifting, even if it was mentally to her work. So he told her to go to it while he cleaned up.

He had things to do as well. And one of them was to talk to Boss and then find them a home. Arryn liked the little place she was living in, but it was very small for someone of his size. Besides, he wanted her to have something of her own too. And he refused to think about how little time there was for them. For now he was going to make things as comfortable as he could, especially for her.

Chapter 5

Jonas looked in the mirror in his room. Right now he was trying to decide if he liked his woman persona or preferred the male, as he was now. Both were very lovely to him, sexy even, but it was the woman that had the others staring at him. He shifted to her body just as the door behind him opened.

"You've been above ground." Not bothering to turn to look at the man behind him, Jonas asked him what he was talking about. "First of all, I can smell the putrid smell of it on you, and secondly, someone saw you coming back. You should take better care when you sneak away."

"I had business to attend to. I have mentioned to you that there is a soul that is mine for the taking, haven't I?" He turned then and showed his breasts to Peter. "Are these too large, do you think, for my body?"

Peter came toward him and lifted them up. Jonas was surprised at the feeling he got from it, but when he let them go with a hard bounce, it was sort of painful. Peter told him that he liked them just fine. Jonas shifted to a man again, thinking he'd go back to his woman figure later.

"This soul you have, does he have a name?" Jonas said it was a girl child and he had no idea if it had been titled or not. "Named. Not titled, but named. And it's female, not girl child. For as much time as you spend up there, you'd think you'd have a better understanding of things. I'll look into things for you. See what I can find out. I might even try a few things while I'm there just to see if I'm as powerful as I think."

"I go there to recruit, not to socialize. And if you go, be very careful. I think she has help, or at least someone there lending her some confidence. She was most rude to me last night when I spoke to her." He sat down near the fireplace and stoked it up more. "You should see how they are. Some of them have no idea what is in store for them. I should like to bring them all down here and see how they manage. And this girl child...female, is no different other than she is mine."

"Is this the female that her mother sold you?" Jonas nodded. "It must be coming close to the end. Have you talked to the girl yet? Have you tried to bargain with her?"

"She'll come around. I know that she will. No one would willingly come here if they had a chance to get out of it. For as much as I love it here, there are just as many who don't care for it." Peter nodded and said he was amazed himself. "I have spoken to her about what I want, but she refuses me. But the closer she gets to her time, I'm sure she'll come around. And if nothing else, I will threaten her with her mother. I don't care for her in the least, but you know the bonds between mother and child. I don't understand humans, but they do serve their purpose."

Both men shivered. Love. That word alone could make him sick to his belly. And he'd run from the room should even one of the others talk about it. It wasn't something he liked to think about.

"She knows you then." Jonas shook his head then looked away. The mother knew him, his name as well as what he looked like in his truest form. He'd been arrogant when he'd gone to her when she called and he'd thought to show off. But now that the girl-child—daughter, he supposed—was coming to him, it would matter little to anyone the grave mistake he'd made. He was going to take the mother too, but no one knew that just yet. He decided to share with Peter now. Not that he fully trusted the other demon, but he might need him for something later on. A scapegoat or something similar sometime.

"The contract has my name on it but little else. My blood of course; as you know, that is how a contract is signed. But she told me that she'd keep it in a safe place, and she wants immortality too much to let that go." He smiled at Peter. "When I told her she may have her life forever, I never told her where she'd have it. I am going to enjoy bringing her to my bed and showing her what I have in store for her. Perhaps you would like a part of her when she arrives. But the girl child...female I have plans for. She will be mine."

"And Damon has approved this?" He hadn't, but then he didn't know about it, so it mattered not a whit to him what Damon approved. "You do know that when he finds out what you've done, he will be angry. I don't think I want to be around you when he finds out. You know what he does daily to that minion, Markum? Lord Damon is not a very tolerant demon when he is pissed."

"I'm not concerned with him finding out." He was, but he wasn't going to let the female out of his room ever, so it wasn't even worth worrying about. "You should see her, Peter. The female has a body that begs to be fucked and a mouth that could suck a cock dry by just looking at it. I am going to enjoy taking her every moment of the day."

They talked more of the woman and the child. Jonas was a man who got things done and never got caught. When he was, he just bought his way out of things or lied. He was the greatest liar he knew. And he had no problems blaming someone else for his crimes, either. Not even good friends. That was what his treasures were for, to use as currency. And it was the only reason he collected so many different kinds. Everyone had a price and Jonas prided himself on knowing it and having it. There was always a price for anything he did, and it was a rare time that he didn't have what the other person wanted. If he didn't, then he simply killed them. It was as simple as that.

The burn on his hand had him looking for something to hide it with. It was happening again. The last time he'd nearly cut his arm off, the pain had been so bad. It wasn't at all like the flames in his pit or the one that he used to heat his home, but a cold kind of burning that made his skin crawl with the need to end it.

"What is that?" He looked at Peter when he stood above him. The pain was so intense that he nearly screamed with it. "You're touched. An angel has touched you. You know those things and their purity can make you catch fire before even a real fire can. Even with just a touch. You said you didn't see anyone when you went there but the girl. What have you done? You'll bring them all here now. See that you don't."

"Shut the fuck up and sit down. There has been no angels in my life. Never that." He held out his hand and watched as the burning moved up his arm. "It cannot be an angel. They cannot come here without permission, and even if I did invite one here, Damon would have felt it too and would be here demanding answers, as he always does. I cannot stand the man. He thinks himself so above everyone else."

"He is above us. Only second to the king. I should tread carefully when speaking of him. It's said that he can hear a pin drop a thousand miles away."

Jonas had heard that as well. He didn't believe it, but he'd heard it.

As the burning stopped, he watched as flakes of his skin, large portions of it, fell off. He held his hand near the fire, something he'd learned the last time it happened, and was surprised that this time it didn't work. The skin still continued to peel away.

"You should tell someone about that. That is nasty." Jonas nodded then shook his head. "Don't ever touch me with that...that thing. I don't know what it is, but I don't want it either."

As soon as he left, which was within seconds after Peter saw his arm, Jonas went to the fire again. This time the skin healed as it had before, but there were still places on it that were white. And that was what concerned him the most. He had heard long ago that when a demon touched an angel things would happen, but he'd never believed it.

He knew that either the woman that had signed the contract was doing this or there was someone there, in the underworld, who was doing this to him. The only way that someone could harm him this way was with his blood. And only a few people, three that he could remember, would have had any of his blood. He had no illusions about the Sharp woman being smart enough to do something like this; Lord Damon, again a person he had no faith in being intelligent enough to think of harming him; and the king himself was too busy getting fat and laying by the fire to do much more than come out once a month for inspections.

Damon might have made the effort if he'd had any idea what Jonas had been doing these last centuries. Markum had some of his blood as well, now that he thought on it. But he knew that the minion would be in too much pain daily to make the effort to torture him. Not that there was a reason for him to think he should try, at least as far as Markum knew about. There just had to be another reason why he was burning like this. There was no way that it could have been just from going above to the other realm. Markum had been able to do it almost daily without this sort of consequences. Then there was the other king…Boss, they called him.

Jonas had been newly turned to minion at that time. Boss had seen him. Jonas had been wandering around the other world trying his hand at recruiting. It had been so long ago that he doubted that He would remember him at all. And back then, Jonas had been nothing more than a speck in His world. But trick him He had, a trick that Jonas now used himself.

"I should like a small sample of your fiber." Jonas had asked Him what that was. "Oh, nothing that you would miss. A spot of your blood. A sliver of your skin. Nothing much. I'm thinking of keeping a log of all the creatures in both worlds. You would be the first that I collect, should you want."

"And what will this give me?" Even then Jonas had been greedy, something he was still cultivating and working on now. "Will I have my name there, as the first of your collection?"

"Yes. I shall put your name at the top of my list." Jonas had put out his hand then jerked it back. "You wish to say no? Oh well, it's fine if you're afraid for me to do this. I will find another that will — "

"I never said I was afraid." The man nodded and smiled, as if He knew that Jonas was actually terrified of what He wanted. "I only want to make sure that you spell my name correctly. I may change it someday, but you will have my real name. The only one that will besides Lord Damon."

Jonas sat down again and though of the blood he'd given the man. And his name. His real name, a name that he could be summoned with. He looked around his suite and thought of it now, and hoped that the man who had it would never remember that He knew something that even Lord Damon never got. It would be his downfall should anyone find out.

~~~

Boss watched the young woman work. She was trying her best to get this figured out for Judith, and He was very proud of the way she was going about it. Having Arryn so close to her all the time had her irritated with him, but she never let her temper go while she was with the others. He looked over at Michael when he stood beside Him.

"You could just tell her." Boss asked him what the fun in that would be. "They could find more time for each other then. You have said that they have had relations. Why have you not hounded him into marrying her?"

"I do not hound anyone. And I will talk to them when it is time. For now they are happy. Or he is. She is coming around to my way of thinking as well." Michael huffed, a habit He thought he'd gotten from Dusty. "Should you like to have a go with her? Talk to her about wedding our Arryn?"

"Nay, I would not. I think I would rather You boiled me in my own salad than me being near her when she is most upset." Boss thought about correcting him on the soup, not salad, part of his comparison, but He loved watching Kala do it. She was nice about it but did tease him well afterwards. "I have heard the words that she said to Arryn and what she did to him when she was upset. Is it true that she can bring down a building with her wrath?"

"It is. However, the part where she brought it down on several people is an untruth. There were only two, and one of them was already dead. Not by her hand." Michael nodded but Boss knew he'd keep his distance from Renie. "Did you hear what Galin has done? He was in a department store with our Kipling buying a gift...well, a replacement gift for Dusty, when he brought down an entire shelf of dishes. There were several hundred of them, I'm told, and he only just put one of them back on the shelf when it happened. Poor man."

"Kipling told me just last night. He said that Dusty told Galin he is to never enter a store without his hands in his pockets. She threatened him with making him sit in the car when she has to shop from now on, too. Did you hear about the eggs?" Boss had and they both laughed. "He is very clumsy. For one so light on his feet when he is working, he is most clumsy with breakable things."

They both turned to the table when Judith laughed. They had missed what was going on, but whatever it was, Renie was not happy with Arryn. She had him lifted up by magic and he now hovered above the table they were all at, saying how sorry he was. Boss decided to make His presence known to them all. Arryn only waved at Him from his height and welcomed Him to the restaurant.

"This would go much quicker if I did not have to look up to speak to Arryn. My dear, do you think it possible that you let him down, for now? I've things to say to you both." Renie looked at Him then at Arryn. Boss laughed, but covered himself quite nicely with a cough when she glared at him. "Please?"

"He said he bought a house." Boss knew this; it was one of the things he'd wanted to talk to them about. "For me. I don't want a house. I want him to leave me alone."

"You do not. And I think you know this as well as I do." Arryn was let down with the warning that he move away from her. "Thank you. But I do need to speak to you both. It is about your contract."

He knew as soon as she looked at Him that she had it. Boss had only been guessing that she'd found the contract between her mother and the man who would take her, but now He knew. And after the conversation He'd had with Arryn about her dream, He had thought maybe she knew more than He did. Now He was sure of it. And He was sure of something else...she knew who the demon was, as well.

"Where is it?" She told Him she didn't know what He was talking about. "I think if you let me read it over that I can bargain for your life. It is not right that I wasn't made aware of the contract in the first place, much less him taking a babe when she could not consent to anything."

"Say I know where it is and what it says...why would it matter to You?" Renie looked away from Him as she continued. "In the large picture of things, I'm not really worth all that much to get Your panties in a twist over. Don't you think?"

"No. I think that you're as worthy as anyone that I watch over. And I have a grand plan for you. Before this...I knew nothing of the contract until I saw you in the courtroom that day." She asked Him how that was possible. "I cannot see into the underworld, and even if I could, what was done to you and how it was done is not right."

"But it's done. Penny will live forever and I will rot in hell." His heart hurt for her. "Arryn will be hurt by this as well, won't he? I think he imagines himself in love with me. Which isn't possible, since we've only known each other for about, what? A day or two?"

"He *is* in love with you, my child." Her pain was raw and real. He wanted to comfort her and took her hand in His. As soon as He did, He realized his mistake. Her scream took His breath away.

Boss held her. Letting her go now would cause her more pain, so He moved His mind into hers and looked for what He wanted. She couldn't block Him out as she dealt with the pain; not that she really could, but He knew the pain it would cause her should He just take the information. So Boss took everything He could from her before He let her go.

Arryn moved Him away from her and took her to his body. As soon as his wings closed around her and they disappeared, Boss stood up. But He fell back, the weakness in His body surprising as well as painful. As He sat there, He let her memories, her pain, run over Him. The demon was going to pay for this as well.

"You going to sit there and scare me witless, or are you going to speak to me?" He looked at Michael, who had not just drawn his sword but looked ready to do battle for Him. "You do not know what it was like for me to see you thusly. Do not do that again, if you please. I'm not a man to be trifled with."

"I shan't. I have what I need." Boss looked at Judith and Dusty, who had drawn their swords as well. He was very proud of them in that moment. "I am fine now. She needed me to see what she would not share willingly. I know a great deal more than I did before."

"And you had to just move in and take it? Even at the cost of harming you both? I do not like this, sire. You have gone too far."

He knew Michael was scared; to be honest, so was He, but Boss knew that Michael talking to Him this way was not going to get them anywhere. Instead of telling him it was enough, He only stood and crossed His arms over His chest. It was enough to make Michael back off.

"I'm sorry, my Lord. I was beyond terrified when she screamed, and then to have You nearly fall…it was more than I had thought could happen."

"For me as well." Swords were put away and Boss sat down as He continued. "We must find out why this has come to be. There are rules to follow and even in the underworld, they are sticklers about such things. And he was there…this demon arranged this entire event to get what he wanted. We do not—either world—go in and manipulate things to have an outcome that we wish. Not ever. I will speak to his lordship and find out what he might know. Can you arrange it—?"

"Whoa your horses there, big guy." He and Michael both looked at Dusty when she spoke. Setting a glass of tea in front of Him, she mimicked His stance from earlier. Her arms weren't quite as big, but He knew her to be powerful. "You're going to go and have tea and crumpets with the king shit himself of the underworld? I thought you guys were...I don't know, sort of mortal enemies."

"There are enemies and then there are rules." She cocked a brow at Him and He had to work hard to not laugh at her. She was a might dangerous when upset. "We each have rules that we adhere to. His are less flexible than mine, believe it or not. And when one is broken—especially after the last encounter we had with his realm—he has been very good about keeping them in line. His minions, I mean."

"You don't call us minions, do you?" He shook His head, but He had feeling that Dusty didn't really believe Him. "Anyway, about this tea and cookies stuff. I vote no. No way in...well, hell...are you going to have a sit down with this guy without me there."

"Nor me." Boss looked at Judith, who had come to him with a plate of cookies. Then he watched as both their husbands came to stand next to them. He was sure had she been able, Kala would have been there as well. He started to speak when Judith continued. "You have to be really smart or really stupid to do something like this. I mean...is it worth it?"

"It is for Reyna." No one spoke, but He could see that they thought it was worth Him going to see the underlord. "I will take the utmost care with him. He is...for all his work, he is a fair and very good man. I'm not saying that I trust him wholly, but I know that once he finds out about this, he will have some words to say about it."

While no one was happy, they did sit with him calmly. Michael went to check on Arryn and Renie as the rest of them sat around the computers that had been left behind. Kipling was staring at the screen when he suddenly stood up and went to the paperwork that Renie had spread out on the desk. Boss looked at Dusty.

"He's getting into helping her. She told him this morning that there was something there, but she was too close to it. As she was explaining to him what she had found so far, all I could think about was how far behind I am in everything." Dusty smiled. "Did I tell you that he's going to advance to the ninth grade? Gifted classes for the most part, and then he'll be able to take some on-line college classes next year."

"That is wonderful news." He looked over at the boy who was going through the paperwork like a tornado. "Renie has a system. Perhaps he should make sure he puts things back before she returns."

"Oh, he will. She's already warned him about her things. She warned Arryn, too, when he moved something to another pile. It was the funniest thing I've ever seen."

Michael returned then and He stood up when he didn't come to the table. "She is awake. Madder than...she is most unhappy with You. And Arryn. I have never seen a person so...all he did was suggest that she have a lying in for a bit before coming back here." Boss nodded, laughing himself. "Lady Reyna can be most...loud, when she is in the mood."

"I'm sure that all of the women can be vocal with their displeasure when they want." He turned back to the group before He continued with Michael. "Will you call in the meeting with the underlord for me? I need to get this taken care of as soon as possible."

"Do you think he is aware of this?" Boss told him he didn't think so and sincerely hoped not. "He will be very angry should he not be aware. Do you think it wise that you speak to him, on his grounds?"

"Invite him here, to this realm." Boss looked around the pretty little shop. "Ask him to come here, to the deli. I think he might enjoy some fine dining after all this time. Make sure that you let him know that it's my treat. For all our riches, we still enjoy having a meal on someone else on occasion."

Michael was still laughing when he left Him. Now Boss had to tell Judith and the others what His plan was, and to convince them that they had to behave. He didn't want a war started over someone trying to kill the king of hell any more than he wanted Renie to be a subject of said king. But they had to talk. There was no way around it.

Sitting down, He started speaking just as Renie and Arryn appeared. He knew that something had happened. He moved toward her, but Arryn stepped in front of Him. That startled Him more than anything.

"She...her magic is beyond...she is very powerful. And has little control over it." Boss nodded and looked at Renie as Arryn continued. "You may wish to speak to her outside, sire. She might feel better, safer anyway, out there. I have a mess...there is a mess in the room upstairs from when all the furniture began to move and fly. My Renie is terrified that she'll hurt someone."

Chapter 6

Renie paced back and forth in the large field as she tried to get her thoughts in line. She was terrified of what had happened upstairs in the little apartment, and now that she was outside in the open, it made what had happened seem surreal. She looked up when Boss said her name.

"Did you know that this would happen? Did you have an idea that this stuff in me would...take over?" He shook his head and then nodded. "Not helpful. I'm scared out of my underwear right now and I'm afraid that I might hurt you. I don't want to, not really, but I might."

"What has happened?" She looked at Arryn to be assured that he was still all right. "Tell me and perhaps I can fix this.

"I nearly killed him when one of the couches upstairs flew across the room and hit him in the head. I had no idea...it just happened, and there he was just lying there." Boss looked at Arryn and Renie felt her eyes fill with tears. "I was hurting and he was trying to help me. But something...I don't know what...it sort of bundled me up and then spit me out. When it did...when it did, all the furniture in the room started to swing around like it was on some sort of circus ride."

"I have told her that I am well. But she was frightened when the blood was seeping from my head." Boss looked at his head and there was nothing there. "I tried to explain to her that I heal—several times, as a matter of fact—and that I am an immortal. But she won't believe me. I think she fears that she might hurt any of us next time and...she wants me to lock her away."

"I fucking will hurt you now if you don't stop talking about me when I'm standing right here." Renie took a deep breath and then let it out slowly, counting to ten as she did. "I'm sorry. I've never had that happen before. I've brought down a building, but that took a lot out of me and then I was out for several days. Right now I feel like I could run...what is wrong with me?"

"What do you know of the men who sired you?" She told him nothing. "There were several, as you know. What you might not know is that they all contributed to your conception. And each of them—well, three of them—had magic. Not very powerful as individuals, but together it was a great deal."

"So I got it. From...how is it possible that I'm here because of several men? I don't understand." Boss nodded and she thought that He was trying to shield her from something. "Just say it, damn it. I've had enough people walking around me like I'm some fainting lily that will keel over if something upsets me."

"I think should anyone spend more than ten minutes with you, Renie, they would change that opinion very quickly. But as for the men.... You have their magic. It was planned that you should have it to...to last longer once you were in the underworld." She sat down. It was simply too much to believe that, first of all, several men were her father and that she was this powerful. "You were to come into it when you turned twenty-five. Your mot…Penny knew it, but it's not why she made the deal with the demon. She was tricked into giving you to him. I believe now that the demon that holds your contract is the one that set this up. He handpicked those men to sire you. Chose them to rape the woman who would bring you life, and then he whispered in her ear that he could give her immortality in exchange for your soul."

"Why?" He didn't answer her and she looked up at Him. "Why did she not give me up for adoption or leave me where someone could find me? Was his whispering so strong, or was it because she was so weak? What is it about my…whatever this is; what is it that scares her enough that she would sell me? Tell me, damn it."

"Both I think. His voice would have been strong enough to pull her there, but her will, her greed is what turned it for you. And because with this magic you'd have it all, while she still had nothing at all." In a sick sort of way she could see Penny thinking along those lines. "I'm so very sorry."

"She would do that, you know. Make someone lower on the ladder of life and fairness that she had in her head; make sure that she was the one with the most. It's why she wanted me to give her my money all the time. She never needed it, her family left her comfortable. But I had it and she knew that I had more than her. Even at the expense of me going without. I did it, too, at first. Gave her everything, until one day I just decided that she was never going to love me no matter how much I gave her. It was never going to be enough." Renie sat there thinking of her lot in life. "I'm in love with Arryn. I think I've figured out that was Your plan, but You had no idea that I was sort of spoken for, did you?"

"Nay, I had no idea until you told me in the courthouse. I have since been looking into it. I have a meeting in a few days to talk to the lord of the underworld to see what he can tell me. I'm sure he has no idea either." She looked at Arryn while Boss continued. He had told her he'd give them privacy because what she had to say was going to be about him. "You have to know this was not my plan when I mated you to him. I didn't know of the contract."

"It says that I can get out of it should I give him a piece of ten protectors. I won't do that, but I want you to know that I can get out of it. For him." She looked at Boss then. "Do you know what he'd do with a piece of them? And what this piece is that I'm supposed to get for him?"

"I do. It's their feather. A feather from their wings. It's as much a part of them as their blood and heart. Should they lose one, they would never be whole again." She asked him what being whole meant. "They would never be able to come to my realm to die. If the demon has it, he has a part of their soul, a part that I have given them. And as for what he would do with them? He would rule them. Command them because of what he is, what he can do. And should he destroy the pieces of them in the pits of hell, then they would burn as well. Forever, child. Not even I could put out the eternal flame that would be set to them."

"I thought they were immortal. I didn't even know that they could be killed at all." He looked away, then at her again. Renie waited, wanting to know as much about the man she loved as she could.

"There are a few protectors, not many, that tire of what they are doing. One of them you know is nearly to that point." She asked him if it was Valyn and he nodded.

"When he comes to me, and I fear he will, Valyn will hand me his medallion and then he will give me a feather. Once I have it, I will not destroy it but will keep it in a safe place. Then I will put him into a sleep so deep, he will be gone from us."

"I see. So you can kill them, but no one else can. But there are other ways to kill them, right? I know that, somehow." Boss nodded and produced a blade so beautiful that it burned brightly in the light of the day. There were markings on it that she knew were magic.

"Yes. They can be destroyed by a blade such as this one. You should know that protectors can kill the lords of the underworld with the same type of blade. My men and woman, all of them, are also armed with such a blade to kill their kind should a war come to pass again. The blade must be used to remove their head. It will not only destroy us but our blades as well, so they cannot be used against us. Same with the protectors. The swords are magical. All the Mystics have one as well, including Dusty and the other women. They work to protect us as much as they do." She told Him that Lily was different than Judith and the others. "She is a protector like Arryn, not a mate to one. I think…I believe it is why she burns you when the others do not."

"She's sort of pure." Boss nodded and Renie thought of something else He might not know. "The man who signed the contract, the demon, that's not his real name. I don't know what it is, but that's not it."

"You're sure?" Renie nodded. "How do you know this? Are you aware of what repercussions this will bring should we figure out that he's lied on a contract?"

"Color me silly, but I thought that was a way of life for his kind." Boss laughed, so Renie smiled at him. "I'm going to die in seventeen days. I lied about my birthday. Not just to you, but to myself too. I know when this ends, and I guess I was trying to pretend like I had more time."

"We will have to work quickly then." She stood up and watched as Arryn came toward them. "He is in love with you as well, Reyna. Very much so."

"Yeah, I have that effect on people." Boss was careful not to touch her, but she could tell that He wanted to. He was a hugger and normally she wasn't, but she thought that she could use one about now. "Can we try something? I mean, if it hurts, just back the...just back up."

"I should very much like to try it. Give me permission, Reyna, and we shall see if I can hug you to me." She nodded, almost ready to tell Him to forget it when she realized that He was laughing at her.

"I would very much like for You to give me a hug if You think You can do it without—" He had her in His arms almost before she could finish the next word. It felt wonderful, like light and bright sunshine. She looked up at Him and saw the tears in his eyes, and they brought her own. "If this doesn't work out, I'm really going to miss you."

"And I you, love. And I you." He wiped at her tears then let her go. "But we will work this out, and when we do, you and Arryn will marry and I can have a new Mystic working with the others."

As they made their way back to the shop, Arryn held her hand. It was a feeling that she'd grown to enjoy. Looking up at him, she knew that of all the people that had come into her life, she would love him and miss him the most of all. Leaning into him, she told him that she loved him.

The next thing she knew, they were in a large room. Arryn grinned at her. There was something very boyish and charming about his smile.

"I wanted you to see our new home." It was on the tip of her tongue to tell him it was a waste of money for him, but she looked around. "This is our room. Bedroom. There is one on the lower level that was intended for the master bedroom, but I love the light in this one. If you should like the bigger room—it's not really that much bigger—but if you should like it, we can move back to it."

Skylights were all over the ceiling and there were large floor to ceiling windows on the back side of the room. Renie went to those. The view was spectacular. It looked right down into an orchard. There was also a large pond back there with a dock and a smallish house near it.

"The pond is stocked, they told me. And it costs very little to have it done monthly should you want to fish. I have never been, but I think it would be a sport that I could enjoy." Renie leaned against him when he wrapped his arms around her as he told her about the view. "I have been here in the evening, while you slept. I needed to be assured that it would be safe for us and the other protectors. There is a family of deer that comes out at dusk. They have a few fawn with them now."

"I've never been fishing either. I'm not sure how much of a sport it is, but I think I'd like to do that too." He held her tighter. "I'm going to die, Arryn. And soon. I'm going to...I don't want to. I've never cared before I met you and the rest of the guys you hang out with. And even Dusty and Judith. But I don't think this is going to end well for me or for you. I just...I don't want to lose you like this."

"We will be able to fix this. I know that we can. Boss is working very hard to make…. I love you too, Renie. I cannot go on without you. I don't know what I would do without you in my life now that you've moved into my heart." He turned her into his arms. "I've asked Boss if I could make you my wife, and He said that we can do this when you are ready. But He would like to wait a few more days. I told Him not much longer than that if He could manage it."

"Make love to me, Arryn. Take me somewhere that means a lot to you and make love to me all night long. And let's not talk about what might be or not." His hand came down over her eyes, and when he let her open them again, he told her here was the place that meant the most to him.

It was the same room, only furnished now. The big four poster bed was right under the windows, and the light of the sun that was going down was making shadows across the snowy white comforter. The furniture was dark wood, matching the hardwood floors perfectly, and the skylights were shadowed in some kind of gauzy material. The entire room looked like a picture of a room she'd had hanging in her old apartment long ago, a dream of hers to have someday.

"I saw it there. One night when you were resting, I wanted to give you something that you'd love, something that we could both love. The house was easy to find with the help of Riss. He is quite the haggler." She grinned at him. "The house has a great many acres, I'm told. And Riss has asked that we allow some of the protectors, if they wish, to come here and fish. I have agreed on the condition that they provide their own bait. Riss has a great respect for worms, did you know that?"

"No, I didn't. Worms?" He nodded and smiled. "I'm betting this will be a story that will make me laugh a lot, won't it?"

"Yes. I believe it will." Arryn stepped back from her and looked down at her. "I should very much like to undress you. Slowly so that I might taste each inch of you that I reveal. And when I have you naked for me, I wish to lay you down on our bed and make slow passionate love to you."

"Yes. Please." He kissed her then, his mouth not just touching hers but making love to it. She could feel his love for her, the way he wanted her. When he lifted his head, she looked at him. "I love you, Arryn the Avenger."

~~~

His need was nearly too much. Arryn wanted to strip her down quickly and take her where she stood. But he knew that she wanted passion, love making, and he was going to give it to her. Walking behind her, he thought of a mirror in front of them, and was happy to see them both reflected in it when it appeared.

Her buttons were tight coming through the small holes, but he enjoyed watching her face as he touched her. Each brush of his hand near her breast, the way his fingers grazed her flesh as he opened her shirt, had her breath catching in a way that did the same to his. As soon as they were undone, all of the tiny buttons no longer mated to their hole, he pulled it down over her arms then off her body.

"I love the way your breasts feel in my hands. The way they fill them, overflowing just enough to make me greedy to take the rest into my mouth." He pinched her nipples with his thumbs and fingers. Her moan had him rocking into her bottom. "These hard peaks are nothing like I had imagined feeling in my mouth. To suckle them, feel then harden more when I do, makes me want more. The way you moan...have you any idea what it does to me? How my blood seems to boil, my heart pounds out of time to the way yours does?"

He undid the front snap on her bra and let it fall to the floor as well. Arryn had never seen something to tiny and lacy before. The stark whiteness of it, the purity of it made him think of clouds in the sky and soft blankets on a cold night. Arryn marveled at how something to tiny and so light could hold such a bounty. As he stood behind her, her breasts bare to only him, he kissed her shoulder then moved to her neck as he slid his hands down to the top of her pants.

These were more difficult for him to manage. First of all, there was a tie and not a zipper or snaps. And she'd tied it in the way that had him frustrated at first, until her hands moved over his. He thought he would need to tear them off her, but she had them undone in seconds.

Taking a step back, he filled his hands with her warm bottom. The muscles quivered in his hands and he wanted to watch them as they tightened and flexed. Pulling the pants down over her hips, he was careful not to take her panties with them. Arryn had plans in removing them in a moment, and that would not be rushed.

Licking a path down her spine, he could taste her need. Her fists were tight at her sides as he nipped at the curve of her spine to her bottom. Arryn kissed the tiny dimples on each side. When the pants were at her ankles, he whimpered a little when she bent to help him; her bottom was right in his face and he wanted to take a large bite of her. When she stood before the mirror with him in only the panties, all he could think about was that she was his. Every part of her, every inch was his to take and to love. When he walked in front of her, he took his time studying each part of her, never touching just yet, but memorizing. Then he leaned in and kissed her again, feeling her own hunger was as great as his. Taking another step back, Arryn had to adjust his cock before he hurt more.

"I wish to feast on you. Taste your cream as it flows from your body." She begged him so prettily that he dropped to his knees in front of her, burying his face into her heat and biting her through the silky material to feel her swollen womanhood between his lips. Before ripping them from her body, Arryn slid his hand under her panties, moved his fingers into her heat, and brought her to the first of what he hoped would be many more releases.

Arryn ate at her voraciously. His hunger for her knew no limits as he pulled her closer, using her bottom to keep her where he wanted her. She tasted of hot sweetness, honey, and her own kind of flavor. Cream ran down his chin, onto his chest as he tried to drink all of her. The more that he drank from her, it seemed there was that much more that he missed.

Renie rocked into his mouth, her fingers in his hair pulling him closer still, guiding him to where she wanted him most. Arryn was glad to help her, for he too wanted her to have the greatest pleasure he could give her. And only then would he take his own.

Flooding his mouth and body with her juices, her screams of release made him want more for her. His own body ached, but it was secondary to her enjoyment. When she jerked him from her, staggering back enough that he held her before she fell, Renie begged him to take her.

Kissing her again, he knew that she could taste herself on his mouth. The thought of them sharing something so intimate made his cock jerk in his pants. Laying her on the big bed, he stood over her as he hurried through his own disrobing, and then cried out when she wrapped her mouth over his shaft. It nearly had him coming down her throat much faster than he thought at all possible.

Making love to her mouth, he closed his eyes. He could easily release this way, fill her with his own juices now if she continued to take him this way. Pulling back, he asked her to lay down and he moved up her body slowly again, this time knowing that when he released, when they released, it would be better than ever before. And it would bond them in a way that would make them one forever.

His body hurt to fill her. His cock was leaking profusely now, his own need so close that he was fearful of not giving her pleasure before he took his own. But as soon as he entered her, filled her to the root with his cock, she wrapped her legs around him and he stilled. It was perfect.

"I love you." She told him that she loved him as well. "I wish that I could stay here forever. Holding you like this."

"Fill me, Arryn." He nodded, moving in and out of her body as slowly as he could. But soon it wasn't enough. He had to come; her own body, her sheath was milking him tightly, and he slammed forward once, then again before she screamed his name, her voice hoarse when she cried out again. Arryn not only followed her over the edge of paradise, but he took her twice more before everything in him shut down and he felt darkness take him even as his body emptied into hers.

When he opened his eyes the room was bathed in darkness. He wasn't sure what had woke him, but when Renie started talking he knew it was her dream again. Touching his finger lightly to her arm, he saw what she was seeing. This time there was no mistaking the creature in front of them as anything but a demon, and a young one at that. And that he was angry at Renie for some reason.

"You hurt me." Renie looked at Arryn then, and he wondered if she was seeing him or simply looking around when the demon spoke again. "What right do you have to harm one that owns you? You will stop this immediately. I will not—"

"Fuck yourself." The demon staggered back when Renie spoke. "Yeah, you heard me, go fuck yourself. I'll do what I want, when I fucking want to, before you think to claim me. I'm here now, not in that place you call home. And I will be for the rest of my free days, and you can just go fuck yourself until your cock falls off."

"I *think* to claim you? I will claim not just you but that lovely body of yours as well. And when I am finished with you, if indeed I ever am, I am going to sell you to the highest bidder and watch as he fucks every part of you until you are no longer fit to be in our sight." Renie laughed and Arryn wanted to tell her that was a bad idea. "You think to mock me, female? I will show you what happens when you treat me like I am a lesser being."

As soon as he started toward her, Renie raised her hands. The demon paused, just for a moment, but it was enough for Arryn to realize he might be slightly afraid of this new Renie, one that fought back. For her to back away from him now would be wrong and he was pretty sure that Renie knew it. She had power over the demon and he didn't care for it.

"Come closer." He shook his head, then lifted his chin at her as if...Arryn thought it was to show her that he was braver than her. "You're afraid of me. And you fucking well better be, too, if you know what's good for you. And if you think once I'm here, in this place, that I'm going to be easy for you to subdue, then you had better be prepared. I'm going to knock you on your fucking ass every chance I get."

"You cannot. I own you." The blast hit the demon in the chest, but all it did, as far as Arryn could see, was push him backward a few feet. "What have you done? Where did you get that? You cannot be a part of...I did not want you to come to this until you were older. You are not older yet."

Renie laughed and looked at Arryn. This time when she winked, he knew that she was seeing him. But when she turned back to the demon, she was all business, a term that had never meant as much to him as it did right at that moment. Renie seemed to know just what she was doing.

"I'm not going to come here without a fight. I just realized how much...well, I realized a great many things this week. And going there to be with you is not going to be as easy nor as fun as you might think it will be. I'm going to fight you with everything I have. And it's looking like I'm going to have a little more than you thought I would too." The demon started to sputter and Arryn wanted to laugh. He was afraid, all right, and a little more than confused at Renie. Then it was as if he knew something that no one else did.

"You've gotten them for me, haven't you?" Renie took a step back...he could almost taste her own fear now.

"Yes. Yes. Yes. You did it. You got them for me. How did you manage it? Did you happen to fuck one of them? Did you…oh, I cannot wait. Give them to me now."

"I don't have anything for you." Renie took another step back when it became apparent that the demon didn't believe her. "I'm not going to either. Never."

"Yes, yes, I can see that you've done it. It will not take all your punishment away, no, but it will be easier on you. Maybe it will. I know that the contract says that it buys your freedom, but we both knew all along that it wasn't going to happen. It wouldn't matter if you got me a hundred feathers from the protectors. I still want you here."

Arryn looked at Renie, then at the demon. Letting go of her arm, he sat up on the bed and watched as she struggled in her sleep. As soon as she woke, Arryn stood up and moved away from her.

"Did you do it? Did you collect the parts of us that would make us not whole should you take them? How many have you collected? You've been around at least that many since you've been here. Is mine in that lot too?" Renie just stared at him, then she stood up. "I asked you a question, please? Did you get what he wanted? I'm assuming that he didn't want as many as one hundred. How many did you get for him?"

She was dressing and he wanted to go to her and demand an answer. But she was speaking low, just under her breath, and it wasn't until she turned to him, her face flooded with tears, that he thought perhaps he might have spoken out of turn.

"Am I far from the apartment over the deli?" He shook his head and she moved to the door. When he reached for her, she hit him in the face with her fist. Arryn fell back, his body not used to having so much pain felt, as if she'd hit him with a tree and not her hand. When he started to rise, she stood over him as if she might hit him again. "Don't you dare come near me again. Do you understand me? Not ever again. To think that...that I...how could you do this to me? How could you believe I'd do such a...? Don't come near me again. Ever."

When he heard the door to the front of the house slam, Arryn got up. He followed her, but he was careful of how close he got to her. She was angry and once she calmed down, he'd tell her what a terrible idea it would be for her to do such a thing if it was in her mind to take them to the demon. It would be better when she was calm, he thought. Then he wondered if she'd ever be that calm again.

Chapter 7

The paperwork was spread out all over the table and the floor. She was nearly to the point where she was going to trash it all and begin again when someone knocked on her door. It was the fourth time in the last hour that it had happened. And like before, Renie ignored it.

Judith yelled at her through the door. "I will break this down if you don't let me in. I'm sick to death of worrying about you. Open the fucking door right now, Renie, or so help me, I will come in one way or another."

Renie started to stand and tell her, again, to go away, but her foot had fallen asleep and she couldn't make it work. So instead of yelling back, which she was sick of doing too, she let Judith steam on the other side. But instead of breaking down the door as she had threatened, Judith used her magic, something that the woman just oozed with, and came in.

"I should be out of here in a few days. I think I have it all figured out about your accounts. Thanks for giving me the information on the other — "

"What the hell is going on?" Renie asked her what she meant. "You know what I mean. Every day Arryn comes by to talk to you, and comes down those stairs again like he's had his heart ripped out. What happened? What did he do?"

"Him? Why do you assume he did anything? Maybe, more than likely, it was all me." Judith sat down at the table and Renie stayed where she was. There were used bowls lying next to her where she'd gotten a bowl of cereal to eat rather than take the time to fix something. And there were several cores of apples, something she rarely ate, but they were there. "I'm kinda on a time constraint here, so why don't you just go back downstairs and leave me to it? Whatever you think or know that happened between Arryn and I is none of your business. I know that might be a hard concept for you to understand, other people not including you in their woes, but it's fine."

"Kala wants you to come and see her. She wants you to see the boys." Renie didn't even bother answering her, but turned back to what she was doing. "They're getting really big. They have doubled their birth weight now."

"I can't do that. And I think you know why." Renie picked up a printout of something she'd been working on and handed it to Judith. "They take the money every two then three days. One the second day they take one percent. Then three days later they take three percent. Not a great deal when you think of it in small terms, but when it's in an account as large as yours and Strategize's, it can add up quickly. Also, there are the other accounts you told me about. All of them are being ripped off. Some less than others, but it's amounting to a great deal of money on the other end."

Judith looked at them but said nothing. When she laid the printout on the table, Renie started to explain the rest to her, but Judith put up her hand. Renie sat there waiting for her to scream at her.

"I've not known you for long. Very little when you think about how long I'm going to live, but you don't strike me as the type of person that would give up easily. What did—and I know it was him—what did Arryn do to hurt you this badly? And before you tell me to fuck off again, I want you to know how impressed I am that you've succeeded in blocking me from looking." Renie looked at the papers in her hand without seeing them. Every time she thought of what he'd said to her, it was like an open wound that someone was pouring salt water in. "Renie, please tell me. I want to help you, and I can't if you don't tell me."

"What the hell?" She got up and found the contract. Handing it to her, Renie stood near the couch while she continued. "It states that if I should get ten pieces of ten different protectors and take them to him, he will void my contract with him and I'll be set free. He's already told me that should I take him a hundred I'll still be his fuck bitch. I didn't even know what the fuck the pieces were until I talked to Boss. He told me that should someone give a feather from them to a demon that they'd not be whole. He also told me about how they would die should the demon destroy the feathers, which I also didn't know, and that you all had swords."

"Boss knows about this then?" Renie nodded at her question. "Do you have any idea what...of course you do...Boss would have told you. What did you tell Arryn when you told him that Boss knew?"

Renie got herself a glass of water. She had no idea how long she'd been out of juice and other things, but she really didn't care at that point. Judith was watching her and Renie just let the tears fall now. It was going to be all over in a few days anyway, what did she care anymore?

But the problem was, she did care. A great deal. And she still loved the asshole even though he didn't deserve it.

"He didn't wait for you to tell him, did he?" Renie nodded. "I see. So he just...I'm not sure how this went down, but I can almost see it. He found out that this was in the contract, and he accused you of taking them from us, right?"

"Not really, but close. I...I have these encounters with this demon. He comes when I'm asleep. And he...I guess you could say that he tells me what a fun time I'm going to have once I'm in his clutches. In great detail." Renie sat down, pulled a napkin from the holder to her nose, and blew hard before continuing. "Arryn can...when he's with me, he can enter the dream too. Sort of as a shadow. The demon apparently can't see him, but Arryn is privy to what is said."

"And that's how he found out about the feathers." Renie nodded. "And this demon? He mentioned them, or something about you collecting them for your freedom, I'm assuming, and Arryn thought the worst of you."

"Yes. Only I never even considered it, before or after I found out what it was he was talking about. He thinks that I'm lying to him." Judith asked her if she meant Arryn or the demon. "Both. They both think that I'm collecting them. And then the demon told me that it mattered little if I had a hundred of them, he was going to keep me anyway. Which I guess I figured all along. Boss knows too."

"What did you...? Never mind. I don't think I'd explain it to him either." Judith laid the contract on the table, then picked it back up. "It says here that your birthday is in less than two weeks. I thought you had more time."

"I lied." Renie stood up. "I have to finish this. It's...I just have to finish this. I don't have a lot of time, as you can see. The money is coming out at the bank, but the addresses don't line up. I think...Kip is helping me narrow it down. Did you know that they're taking money from not just yours and Strategize's, but your personal accounts as well? We're talking several million dollars."

Judith didn't look like she was going to pay attention. Renie knew that she was upset about her leaving them. It was the way she thought of it now; not dying, but she was leaving them. When she finally picked up the printout, Renie let go of the breath she'd been holding.

"Did you tell Dusty and the others yet?" She said that she hadn't. "We need to get together and see what we can figure out. How long will it take you to get the right address? And by that, I guess you mean the computer that is doing this."

"Yes. It's not the bank at the local level. I've been using Dan, who has also been a great help; he's gone in and helped me get the IP of all of the ones there. So it has to be either at the main office or another one of the smaller banks. And when I look to see a physical address, it bounces." Judith asked her what that meant. "They have a program on their computer that makes it so the address where the information is being taken from is bounced all over the world. It makes it nearly impossible to find where it originated from. One second it could be here, the next in China, then around the world again in seconds. It's hard to trace, but I'm working on that too."

She took her into the bedroom and showed her what she'd been doing. It wasn't like she'd been using the bed anyway for the last week, so she'd set up computers all over the room. There were nine on the bed and three more on the dresser. And four on the floor.

"I had no idea that…this is costing you a fortune." Renie shrugged and let it go. She was glad that Judith did as well. "What are you doing? I'm assuming that you're chasing the bounce."

"Sort of. What I'm doing is cutting out the bounce. Every time it hits a place, one of these will tell me if it's a real place or just a spot that the computer picked. I've been able to cut out about four million jumps since I started." Judith whistled. "Don't be too impressed. A bouncer can have as many addresses as there are number combinations. I'm just working it to see what I can hit."

As they moved out of the bedroom, Renie looked around. She'd been a slob the last few days, not even picking up her wads of trash that didn't even come close to the trashcan. Judith smiled at her when she said how sorry she was.

"I don't care what kind of mess you have so long as you find who is robbing me. And I expect a bill for those computers too. There is no reason you should be out all that money." Renie looked away and Judith brought her face back around. "I'm assuming since you didn't ask for any money that you can afford this and more. How much…can I ask you how much money you have?"

"More than you." Judith nodded. "I'm not stupid. And I'm good at what I do. It's why I get hired by people like you, and I don't work for a firm. I did once for about a week. But they had little for me to do after I cleared up their mess. I was paid well for the rest of my contract, and I invested even better. I'm good to have around, but too expensive to have on your payroll."

"And you don't want your mom...Penny to have it." Renie shook her head. "Smart girl. But I'm still paying you for this. And your time. I don't know what the going rate is for a computer genius like you, but I'll get it figured out."

"Give it to your foundation. The computers too when I'm...when I have this figured out." Judith said that she'd work something out. As she started to close the door, Judith came back in. After a quick hug, Renie was alone again.

"This was much easier when I was alone. I didn't have any attachments to hurt me when...when I left." She went back to the piles of papers and stared at them. It was harder now; after knowing all these people, it was harder than it had been before. Being alone had been a comfort, a way for her to bury herself into her work, but now it was nothing more than being lonely. And Renie hated it.

~~~

Arryn stretched his neck twice before he heard the pop that he'd been seeking. His neck, along with the rest of his body, hurt. But it was a small price to pay for what might happen today. Riss had offered to let him work in the ring with a couple of the younger protectors. It had been...enlightening, as well as slightly painful. In a good way though.

The meeting that they'd been working on was finally going to happen. Today, he might be able to go to Renie and beg her to forgive him and to marry him. He'd been not just wrong about what she'd been about to do, but a great many things as well. And he had it in his head that she might not ever forgive him, but he would still work to have her free to live her life.

"You have to hold onto your temper, Arryn. If you let it go now, there will be hades to pay." Michael had told him this now four different times. And each time he never got it quite right. "I'm aware that this is hades and we are talking about it, but I'm nervous as well. You would do well to remember that I have said this is a terrible idea."

"I know. And I thank you for coming along anyway." Arryn got up to pace and sat when Boss cleared his throat. "What if we meet him here and then he tells us that's he's too busy to see us? He could, you know; he's done it before."

Five times, as a matter of fact. And today, today he had to have something to go to Renie with. Her time was running out. And thanks to him being stupid he'd lost all this time with her. He glanced at Boss when He laughed.

"She looks no better than you do. Maybe just a little worse. Did you know that she could ill afford to lose any more weight, and yet she has? Poor thing. I do hope that we can help her out with this. But you are on your own with your troubles with her." Arryn knew that as well. Boss had been extremely…well, the man had been pissed off, as Dusty was fond of saying. And none of the others would speak to him since he'd told them what he'd done. Except for Riss, and it had only been to scream at him for being a fool.

"I have tried to see her. Every day she turns me away. Not that I don't deserve what she is doing, but I hurt from it." Boss nodded and leaned back in the seat He was in. "I cannot believe that I said those things to her. I don't even know why I said them. As the words spewed from my mouth, I knew them to be untrue. She would never betray us in such…in any way."

"I think you were scared too." Michael looked at Boss before he continued. "Or you might have been cursed. There is a lot of that going around, I'm told."

"I told you that it was a joke, Michael. Kip was joking with you. If you do not learn to take them, I'm going to forbid you hanging around with that young man. He only does it to make you insane with odd thoughts." Boss looked at him. "Last week they were watching a program on television. Michael asked Kipling how they had made the actor in one movie appear in the next one alive again. They were watching a marathon of something. I don't remember. But Kipling told him that they cursed every actor in movies so that they would be able to come back and make reunions; or in this case, a second movie."

"And you believed him." Michael nodded, saying that it was true. "No, I'm sorry, but it's not true. You know as well as I do that people age and die. And actors aren't any different. I'm sorry."

"Young Kipling said as much to me this morning. I do enjoy the young man, but there are times when I'm sure that he's pulling my wanker." Arryn looked at Boss and then back at Michael. "I know that it's leg. But Kipling assured me that I would get a better reaction with people if I used that term. I have no idea what part of my body is a wanker, and he was laughing too hard to tell me, but I do believe it had the desired effect."

"I think I'm going to have a talk with our Kipling. He might be going too far in using you as a source of humor. I do love him, but this is...perhaps it will be best if you should stay away until I have a word or two with him." Just as Boss spoke, humor spilling from His mouth, a man came into the dining room with them.

The store was closed now; Judith had said that they could lock up after they left. But Arron had a feeling that none of the protectors or Mystics were very far away. He would even bet that there were a few of Dan's crew that were close at hand too. But the man in front of them resembled a large...Santa Claus.

"I don't get out much." Boss nodded and so did Arryn. "I did try to find something that would show I was here in good faith and willing to listen, but this is the image that came up when I put in trustworthy to all. What is this thing?"

"It's a jolly old elf," Boss answered him. Lord Damon shook his body, and he looked like a banker. A very tall one, but also well dressed and groomed. "Much better. And if you don't mind my saying so, very much the way most men dress when going to a meeting."

As they sat down, Arryn noticed that the room changed. It was no longer the dining area of Judith's restaurant, but now a nice living room setting. And it had warmed up a few degrees too. Arryn had not thought of the differences in the temperature that the man would have to endure and smiled at him. As drinks were brought to them and a tray of small sandwiches was left, Lord Damon looked at Boss.

"I have done some research into your...this problem. And I've done some looking on the name that you gave me as well. To be honest, it was cleverly done by whoever did this, but not anything that I was aware of. I do not work that way." Boss told him that he hadn't thought so. "The young woman, you say that she's had contact with my demon? Does she know his name?"

"She has the contract, but she said that she knows that the name on it is a lie. I'm sure you know that we don't work that way either."

Lord Damon looked at Arryn before speaking. "You are in love with her." Arryn nodded. "You're here to do what then? Trade your life for hers should I go ahead with the contract?"

"I would." He didn't even think about it. In fact, it had never occurred to him until then that he could have done that. "If it would save her life, then I would bow before you to save her."

"It won't be necessary. But you should tell her that before much longer. I believe the girl to be ill. Sick with her love for you as well." Arryn didn't even try to figure out how he knew they'd had a fight, but nodded at him. "There is something you can do for me. And I will talk of it later with you. Alone."

Michael stood up and then disappeared. Boss started to stand as well, but Lord Damon asked him to please be seated. He asked that He give him a moment to explain, that it was very important.

"You know what he is to me. You know what Michael is." Lord Damon nodded. "If you have harmed him in any way I shall—"

"I have only sent him to the house of Riss. He is safe there. But he is…you know how he can be when things are not by the book. I was just trying to save us some time. And there is very little of that left, I believe." Boss nodded and leaned back in the chair again. "I thank you. Now the girl. I need the contract. I shall not take it, but I would like to see it. Perhaps I can see something on it that you cannot."

Boss snapped his fingers and Renie was suddenly there. Arryn stood up to touch her, but she backed from him. The fury on her face made him want to both run and hide and pull her into his arms and hold her forever.

"What the fuck? I was in the middle of...who the hell are you?" Lord Damon laughed but he didn't speak. "You're...there is something about you, something...well, I'm sorry, but there is something bad about you."

"Precisely." He stood up and reached for her hand, then withdrew it quickly. "You have been cursed, haven't you? I would say...whoever did this to you did not want you to have help from anyone. Especially anyone that might be able to save you, including me."

"She burns us as well when we touch her. But not Arryn here. I don't know what it is...oh, but when you ask for permission, she can be touched, but I felt the heat of it." Lord Damon nodded. "What is it? Is it one of your curses? I don't believe it is since you seemed surprised by it. So who might it be?"

"I have a thought or two who it might be. And, no. It is the work of one of mine but not me. And it would seem, as much as I hate to admit it, love does indeed conquer all. Nasty business, love." Damon looked at Arryn. "You have hurt her then, because of his curse."

"Yes. I'm not sure if it was the curse or not, but I did hurt her."

Renie whistled then; put her fingers in her mouth and made a sound so loud that he had to cover his ears. Lord Damon only laughed.

"I'm right here. I really hate the way you guys talk around me as if...." Renie looked around. "Where am I anyway? And you never said who you were."

"Lord Damon, second to the king of the underworld. And you are here, on your own realm, in a place that I believe is a sandwich shop owned by a friend of yours." Arryn nearly laughed when Renie didn't seem the least bit impressed. "You are a wonder, are you not? But this curse…I should like to touch you. I may be able to find out for sure who has put it there."

"No." Lord Damon cocked a brow at her but didn't speak when Renie continued. "I'm not sure what you think you can accomplish with touching me. But you might…what if I hurt you? You could do worse to me than that shit head that owns my soul. And if it's all the same to you, I'd just as soon not have my time here shortened because you got a little scorched by me."

"I will not harm you in any way. Nor will I shorten your time here with those that…love you." They stared at each other for several minutes, long silent minutes, before Renie put out her hand. When Lord Damon touched his finger to her, he, as had the others, flared up in flames, but kept touching her. When Renie staggered back, Lord Damon did as well and fell into the chair he'd been in. Arryn took Renie into his arms and held her.

"Do you know who it is?" Lord Damon nodded at him but continued to stare at Renie. "And can you do something about this? See what we can do to get her back?"

"I should like to see the contract, if you please." Arryn went to retrieve it for Lord Damon, and he also got Renie a glass of tea. Lily had told him that something sweet would heal most anything magical. That didn't lessen his worry for her, but he knew that in this, he could be of help.

Arryn handed it to him and Lord Damon looked at Renie. When she nodded, the demon lord took the papers and then looked them over twice before he seemed to understand something on it. Also, Arryn thought the man was upset, but not at them. When he sniffed the blood, the fingerprint of the person who had signed it, he handed it back to Renie.

"I should like to know how you came to have this. I'm assuming that you were not given it by this...Penny person?" Arryn started to ask what difference that made when Renie answered him.

"Penny had it, and when she wanted some money...I went there and took it in trade. I doubt I'll see the money again, but she can have this when I'm paid. I'm thinking I might already be dead when that happens." Lord Damon told her not necessarily. "I don't understand. I mean, you do know that I've only a few days to go yet. And when I turn twenty-five, I'll be in your neck of the woods. What possible reason can you have to think that this might not come to pass? And please give me at least a glimmer of hope. I could really use it."

"The contract is a good one. I will give the person that much. But you must know, and I'm sure that your lord here will back me up, I do not work this way. Nor does my king." No one agreed or disagreed, and for some reason Lord Damon thought that was funny. "I see that we have a few non-believers here. Regardless. The contract will be fulfilled, but you cannot fill it. Unless you want to?"

"No. I mean, no offense, but I'm kinda liking my life the way it is for the moment." Lord Damon nodded. "I don't understand. If you say it will be fulfilled and not by me, who will?"

"Let me tell you something first. And you should know that as much as it pains me, I owe you both a big apology. I came here thinking that this was going to be a slam dunk, as you call it. I would see the contract, know that it was true to the letter, and take you with me. I was...let us just say that I am rarely wrong about people, and for this, I am sorry." Arryn took Renie's hand and was glad once again that she didn't fight him. "But I do need for you to...fulfill it on one level. I should like to catch this...well, I will say in this case, the two of them. The one that cursed you, which is separate from the contract and more than likely unknown to the person who made the deal with Miss Sharp, and the person who is the blood on the bottom there."

"It's not the name on the contract." Lord Damon shook his head and asked her how she knew. "You're going to think this is strange, and after my life for the last several months, that's saying a lot, but I could feel it was a lie. Even before...even before my magic or whatever it is came about, I knew that it was a lie. There are two other things in it as well that aren't true."

"Such as?" Lord Damon leaned forward when she showed him the paragraph about half way down the page. "Ah, yes. That would also be a lie. We do not make bargains for one's soul like this. And had you brought him the pieces of the protectors, I can assure you that I would have known, as would my king. That is something that...it is something that we cannot do to each other without a war. And as much as I enjoy a good war, this is not worth having one over. Not like this."

Lord Damon looked at Boss and they both smiled. Arryn was sort of afraid. And when they both stood up, he knew they were going to leave them. But the demon turned to him. It was the smile that made him think that he was in a lot of trouble.

"As I was saying to you earlier, you and I need to talk. Now is as good a time as ever, I believe. You are human, or are for the most part; did you know that?" Arryn told him no. "You are while you are in her presence because she drains you…you're just enough human, and she is more like you. It balances you both, so that you are neither one nor the other but both. And she is a woman as well. It does not happen often that someone that wrote such a clever contract would miss that, but for now, you are both about as human as you can get. You should take care of making yourself very human."

"I don't understand. That wasn't very clear at all." He smiled and then he disappeared with Boss. Arryn looked at Renie. "Do you know what he's talking about? Balance? Human? I just…was he trying to be confusing?"

"No. I think…I hate to say this, but I think you're all nuts. And I didn't get to tell him the other lie on the contract either." The voice that echoed around the room surrounded them. Apparently he knew what it was too. "This is the most fucked up thing I've seen a long time. And I need a nap. I'm…that was exhausting."

"I'd very much like to take you upstairs and hold you." When she nodded he picked her up. "And perhaps we could make love too. I think that would be a good way for me to show you just how sorry I truly am."

"That is a great idea." They were halfway up the stairs when she stopped him. "We might have to clean up a bit. I've been…working."

He didn't care if it took them the rest of the night to clean up, she was back in his life. And he was never going to mess up like he had again. Never for so long as he lived.

Chapter 8

Jonas rubbed his hands together. Just three more days and he'd have it all. Not only would he have the woman where he wanted her, but he'd have the pieces of the protectors as well. Fourteen she'd told him. Fourteen protectors at his mercy. And then the grand prize that he'd not even counted on.

He'd been surprised when he entered her dream state and she seemed to be waiting for him. Before he could begin his nightly tormenting, which he had enjoyed more than he'd thought he would, she'd spoken to him.

"I have what you want." Jonas had asked her what she had and why he would need whatever it was. "The pieces of the protectors. You could have told me what you wanted instead of fucking being so slick. Just say feathers next time. It will make it easier to figure it out and I won't have to spend time researching for it. Moron."

"It is not as much fun to just say what you want when you can be…slick, as you called it. And you really do have them? How many?" She nodded and he had smiled at her. "You do remember me telling you that I was not going to honor that part of the contract, don't you? I have no use for the feathers, and only put it in there so that you'd have hope. I love it when my victims have hope."

"So you've done this before? This taking babies without their permission?" Jonas had nodded, thinking what did he care if she knew that he had taken over two dozen souls this way. "And their parents, what did they say to you when you came to collect? Did they try to renege on the deal?"

"They came as well. Just as your mother will. I make these deals with desperate people, but I cannot let them tell others of my plans. What would happen should others find out about my ideas? Everyone would want to do it." The woman told him he was a sick fuck. "Why thank you. I do believe that is the kindest thing someone has said to me in a very long time."

"Whatever. I want one thing from you." Jonas had laughed. She was in no way able to bargain with him. He was the one in charge, not this slip of a human. "When I come to you, I wish to be there when you show the parts of the protectors to your partner. He should be there just for the jollies of it."

"I think that can be arranged." It wasn't until later—a whole day later—that he realized she knew about Peter. And now, because of the other bargain she'd struck with him, he could not go to her again or the last feather, the one he was excited to get, would not be his. And the lord of all the heavens' feather was one he wanted more than anything. He thought of the way she'd worded her last demand and wondered several times if she'd had help. A woman did not have the knowledge that she did.

"You will leave me to my peace until six o'clock on the evening of my twenty-fifth birthday in this time zone. And if you do, I will give you the fourteen feathers that I have plus the one that I got just today. The feather of Boss." He'd nearly told her to show him, but he knew that in her dream state, that was not going to happen. "If you break any of these demands, not only will you not get the fourteen, but you won't even see the last one. The one that I treasure."

He had said yes, even told her that he'd not bother her mother either, but she said that he could do whatever he wanted to her. She had made him swear on his life, swear to her that he would do as she asked or everything, the entire deal, was off. And now six days later, he had only to wait two and a half more and he'd be the king of the underworld. Looking up when someone knocked on his door, he nearly hugged Peter to him when he came in.

"It's to work. I cannot tell you how happy I am that you helped me with the contract. Should you not have thought of the pieces of the protectors, then we would not be getting the grand prize of all." Peter listened to him as he told him what she'd said. "And to have the one of their king? We will be envied by all."

"You told her of me?" He said that he hadn't but she had guessed. "Did she say anything else about me? About any kind of problems that she was having? I swear to you, Jonas, if this comes back to bite me in the ass, I will tell everything that I know and even lie to get you into trouble."

Jonas thought it an odd question about the problems she was having but told him that she had not. "You wouldn't even put your name on the contract, so I've no idea why you're so upset. But as I have promised, I will share in my wealth when we're presented before the king. He will be so impressed with us."

"You think so?" Jonas assured him he was positive. "I should have told you this before, but I have put a curse on her. Not a big one, but when you told me who she was, I found out that she was around the protectors. And since we both know what kind of do-gooders they are, I made it so that they'd not be able to help her. No one can help her, not even Damon."

Jonas was surprised that Peter even knew how to do a curse, but thought it a brilliant plan to keep her safe for them. And he told his friend over and over how much they were going to gain from this. He even told him that he wished he was that smart as well. Not that he trusted him. He'd been in this business long enough to know that you trusted no one, sometimes not even yourself. But the man might come in handy later, and he wanted him close.

"The curse, what does it do? I don't want to be pulled into it should I happen to trigger it." Peter told him what he'd done and what would happen if someone touched her. "So the day that you were here and I was burning, you knew why even then."

"I thought I knew but I wasn't sure. I didn't know that it would harm you as well." Jonas only nodded, thinking that Peter had betrayed him one too many times. "You are well now, so what does it matter? And as you have said, she is safe for us."

After Peter left, Jonas sat down in his easy chair. It wouldn't be long now and he'd have it all. And he'd only just decided that Peter was going to have to go. He had no idea how to kill a demon such as himself without everyone knowing who did it, but his days were as numbered as the woman's. Feeling his temper getting the better of him, Jonas thought of the other changes that were about to happen because of her coming here and what she was bringing to him.

Lord Damon would be out and Jonas would be in charge of everything down here. There would be changes then, good ones that would, of course, benefit him. And he thought that might be a way to get rid of Peter, just as Damon had gotten rid of Markum. Jonas might even have a sit in with the king. Excited now, he went to the room he'd had prepared for his captive.

Jonas had no use for the older woman. But he did know that humans, especially human daughters, would do anything for their mother. They loved their mothers no matter what they did to them. He'd known one such mother that had sold her daughter to a great many men, but when it came to it, the daughter had asked to take her place when it came time to collect her for him. Of course he'd taken them both...it was his first adventure into contracts. So he was going to use the older woman to show the daughter just what he had planned for her. And he had a great many plans.

The room he had set up was thick stone. He'd forged it himself over the years, learning a lesson the hard way. Screams, it seemed, could echo down long hallways and bring any matter of others to his room. Sharing his prize was something that he hated doing, and had worked very hard to make it so it never happened again. Especially not with this woman. Never would anyone touch her but him until he was finished with her. And Jonas thought it would be ages before that happened.

Jonas was still worried about the contract. If anyone were to find it he was sure that it would have repercussions that he'd feel for a long time. Just thinking of Markum had him terrified, and he made his way to the house of the mother again. This was his third such trip to the house of the woman, and he hated it more and more each time.

The house was a mess, as it usually was. The woman—Penny, he knew was her name—was sleeping on her couch. Jonas avoided her and looked around the large place trying to sniff out his blood. Each time he'd been there before, he'd known just where it was, but now it didn't seem to be in the house. He wondered if the fool had destroyed it. Then he smiled.

If she no longer had her copy of it, then he could say whatever he wanted about it. He did wonder again how the daughter had figured out the pieces of the protectors. But the mother would have had to prove to her that she was indeed going to be his play thing and might have shown it to her. As far as Jonas could remember, the contract had been in the house well after he'd started visiting the girl.

When it didn't seem it was in the house he made his way back to his lair. Warming up by his fire, Jonas thought of all the things he could say about the contract and a way to get more than he'd wanted. He was already getting a good deal more than he ever thought he'd get, but why not get more? More was infinitely better than less.

~~~

"Explain to me again, and with more detail than you did before, how you think this is going to work. And no more laughing when I ask you something. I have a headache and you're not helping." Boss touched His finger to her head and it was gone. "Thank you. But that does not mean You're off the hook."

"You should be more trusting, Reyna. I've got this under control." He grinned at her. "Have you been sleeping better or have you been up all night?"

Renie flushed and didn't even glance Arryn's way. The man seemed to be insatiable. Not that she wasn't enjoying every second of it, but she had no idea where he was getting his energy. Of course, he had reminded her last night that he'd never had sex before until her, and he had to make up for lost time. She thought he was making a pretty good dent in it. She thought of something she wanted to ask Boss. After kissing her on the forehead, Arryn told her he would return. He was needed, it seemed, at Riss's home.

"What will happen to Arryn if I...if you can't...if this doesn't work?" Boss told her it would. "I don't mean to burst your bubble there, Big Guy, but rarely do things work out the way I need for them to. I've a long list of shit that I thought was right, then it was gone in seconds."

"Your other job, you mean? The one where you had to turn them in rather than let it go on? I think you did the right thing, if that matters to you." Renie nodded. "The men who had hired you to work for their firm thought that you'd be so stuck in your work that you'd not notice just where the money was coming from. They had...well, like most I know...thought you'd be a computer genius but nothing more. They were not expecting you to have a brain as well."

"I'm thinking I might have picked the wrong line of work to go into. But then it sort of picked me, not the other way around." He only laughed again. "You know, I've known You for all of a month now and I'm willing to bet You don't laugh all that much. Or at least understand humor. You think the strangest things are funny."

"Sometimes life can be funny. Like this matching of you and Arryn. Had I known about you sooner and what it was going to bring to the table, I might have—"

"Left me to my own devices?" She looked away when he seemed shocked. "I've not had the best of lives. I mean, I've got a lot of money and I can get anything I want with just a click of a computer key. I won't, but I could. I've a mother, though she doesn't care for me, good friends that I'm going to miss terribly if this doesn't work out. And I have a lover, one that I've only just discovered, that You know that I love very much."

"And he loves you. Reyna, look at me please." She turned to look at Boss and could see that she'd hurt Him with her words. "I would never have left you to your devices. You are mine and I shall have you back into my fold soon now. What was done to you...well, it was not right. To more than just your soul, but to your quality of life as well. No one should know the date of their demise. Especially like you found out."

"What will happen to me when this is finished?" He smiled at her. She didn't like that smile any more than she did a lot of things He'd told her lately. "If this thing with Lord Damon—who I have to admit seems like a pretty straightforward guy—if it works out, what am I going to be doing? I'm assuming that You have some sort of plan for me?"

"I do." He sat there for a long moment. "And I will not tell you. You should know by now that all things come to those who wait. I don't know which of my people said that first, but it is a good thing, don't you think?"

"Not particularly. No, I don't." He laughed again. "I'm serious. Will I need to find something to do? I have to stay active and working. I'm not a very good idol person. Devil's workplace and all."

"You are something else. And I think you will be a great addition to my Mystic's." He leaned back in the chair. "You will work with the group. I believe there are things that you can do from here that we can use on other projects. Nothing illegal or anything like that, but there are things you can do. And I know that you will have the offer of a very well-paying job, but with a firm that you can trust from a man that I trust. We will be purchasing more buildings in the future. And though we will pay for them, it will help us on occasion to have the paperwork moved quickly. You can do that. Some of the protectors have funds; some a great deal that will need to be moved from the current currency to something more manageable."

"Such as?" He told her. "I see. So you pay your people in gems and gold, and it needs to be turned into hard cash? I can do that. But it will…some places charge a percentage, so it might not translate to be the same amount. I don't want anyone to think that I'm trying to rip them off."

"Do you know how long some of the men I have working with me have been saving?" She told Him that she had no idea. "Arryn has been saving for more millennium than most. He and Riss are not the oldest, but very near. Tholan, who you have met, has been with me longer than those two, so his worth would astound you."

"So you're saying they have a lot of stuff to change over and won't miss a few bucks of it." He told her He doubted any of them knew their real value. "Everyone should know their real value when it comes to money. It makes you know just…well, I'm guessing if you live forever you really don't care if you have enough for retirement, do you?"

"Not really. But some of them…a lot of them have come here, to this realm, to rest and relax. In doing so, they have found that they enjoy some of the other things that are here. Movies, having a home to go to." He waved his hands in front of him and a neat little house appeared. "This house is one that Valyn has his eye on. It is not without its problems…plumbing and a new furnace…but he has no idea how to work on the purchase price."

"I can do that for him. Just give me the address." He said that He would. "There is more too, isn't there? I mean, more than just a few houses and money changed over?"

"There is. I have a great many things I'd like for you to teach the men and women that work for me. Not just how to use the computer, but how to look at it when one of their charges are at it. There have been times, I'm sure, that they might have missed something important because they didn't know how to guide them in the right directions." She asked Him if He meant something they might have been searching for. "That and other things. I've had…well, we've had a few conversations about it, and I believe that you can help me out by teaching a class at the compound. You would do well in it, I think."

"If this thing works out." He told her not to worry so much. "Yeah, but I'm really good at it. You should know that by now."

After He left her, she moved to her makeshift office again. The computers were running all the time now and had displayed a list of places longer than she was tall that were not real addresses. She sat down at the one closest to her and began reading the reports on it. There were so many that she really could not believe that a single person had set this up.

When the address for the house that Valyn wanted came to her, she moved out of the program and to the house listing. It was there for her to do a virtual tour, and she could see that it needed more than just a little work. As she continued she made a list of things that were going to need to be fixed and updated. By the time she was done, she had a long list of not just the repairs, but the cost of them as well.

Calling to Valyn brought him to her almost immediately. His face was serious, as it seemed to be a great deal, and when she asked him about the house, he looked like he had no idea what she meant.

"Aren't you interested in a house on Mullen Street?" His face cleared up then as he nodded. "Okay. First, tell me what about this house makes you want it? Because I have to tell you, the place is nearly falling down now."

"It is a small house that I have enjoyed looking at from afar. You have been there then?" She told him about the tour she'd taken. "I'm not...I have not been on a tour of it. Just saw it from across the street when I had a charge there. I will admit that it was a long while ago, but I think that I will have the funds to fix things."

After setting him up with the computer and the online tour, she went to the kitchen to make herself some tea. She was so thirsty all the time, and she hated the fact that it was sweet stuff that seemed to quench her thirst. When he joined her in the kitchen with the laptop, he told her that the house was not what he had expected.

"I didn't think so. But you can look from here to find one. I have two friends that are agents that can help you. One of them is a real bastard, but he owes me. The other...well, she's a little off at times, but she will be honest with you." He asked her the names and she told him.

"The female is a protector that has retired. She is honest, yes, because she cannot be anything but that. The male, I do not know. Why does he owe you?" Renie told him. "You saved him from going to jail for tax fraud, and you say that I can trust him?"

"I said he owes me, so he knows better than to mess with me again." Renie grinned. "I bought a house from him a while back. He tried to tell me all kinds of things about it that weren't true, and a few things he tried to keep me from knowing. They have to tell you everything about the house you're buying or it comes back to bite them in the ass." Valyn told her that was why he never liked humans on a personal basis. "Then why are you buying a house to live among them?"

"I should like a place that is far from people, if possible. I know that the first house was not it, but I should like one that has many acres. Also, a large house that I may wander around in, fixing things as I see fit." She nodded, making mental notes on his wishes. "There is such a house that is not far from here. But it is in the courts now and will be there for a long while yet. I do think that the family enjoys fighting over everything."

"I think you might be right on that. I've known a few people that argue even if they know that they're wrong." He nodded and looked at the computer in front of him. "Put in the address of the house you really like. Maybe I can dig around and see how much longer it's going to be."

Two hours later, Valyn was making an offer on the house, and ten minutes after that, he was the owner. She had made good on her promise to convert his money, and as soon as he made his way to the bank to get the paperwork, he could move in. Valyn looked like he was happy, but she didn't worry about him any less. His heart seemed to be…not there anymore.

Not only was the house in good shape, but the bank had taken it about a month before the previous owners had died. The family, it turned out, was fighting over something that didn't even belong to them, and they even knew that going in.

After talking with the banker, then the attorney working on what was owed on the house versus what they needed to part with it, it was established that he could put an offer on it. Valyn was so happy with her that he hugged her several times before he left for the bank.

"You have done well for him." Renie jumped when Tholan spoke. He'd not been there a second ago and now he was. "I should like for you to help me with something as well. If you would be so kind."

"You don't like me much, do you?" He only stood there saying nothing. "Okay, I'll help you, but you have to tell me why you hate me."

"I do not hate you. I do not even know you." She told him that was his fault and he flushed. "I will not bother you again."

"You leave here and I will hunt you down and beat the living crap out of you. Sit." He nearly fell over in his haste to do as she'd told him. "Now. We're going to do this my way. Tell me why it is you don't care for me."

"You have much going on in your life." She asked him what that was supposed to mean. "I do not know…I just…I am jealous of all that you can do and the ease with which you can perform it."

"You think this is easy for me?" He nodded and flushed again. "Okay, first of all, none of this is easy. Even the computer stuff that I can do, it's not always cut and dry. Sometimes it takes me weeks to get a simple task to go the way I want it to, then longer to set it up again so that it works correctly. I have all kinds of stupid shit going on in my personal life that I'm very sure you're aware of, and then there is you."

"Me?" She nodded at his squeaky question. "I have done nothing to you. I have avoided you at all costs since you have come into our lives."

"And that's the problem. You make me feel like I'm not worthy of being your friend." He swallowed twice before asking her if she thought of him as her friend. "I'd like for you to be. I've seen you with Kala and the other women and you act...well, not at ease, but nice around them. And with me...well, it's like you said, you avoid me at all costs. I didn't do anything to you."

He got up to pace and she realized that this was something that they all did...pace themselves into a corner rather than just saying whatever it was that was bothering them. Renie stopped him and told him to tell her what was on his mind.

"I am in awe of you. And I fear you too." She asked him why. "Because you can do more with that device than I can with my entire stack of notebooks and their notes. I will search for hours for one little word to see if I am using it correctly, and you just punch a few keys and there it is. What I would not give to have such a talent as yours. And it does not end there. You can do most anything you set your mind to."

"I can help you with that. Download a dictionary and thesaurus to your computer. We can transfer all your notes over easily enough by just copying them to a file. It won't be hard." He was shaking his head. "You can do it all on your own. It will take you a while, but I'm sure that with some help from your friends you can do it. You're not stupid, Tholan, just ignorant of the process. There is a big difference. I can show you how to get started and from there, it will take a while like I said, but you can input all the notes you have, even make a schedule on the computer and have it all at your fingertips."

"You would do that for me? Even after the way I have treated you?" She nodded and told him it would be her pleasure. "You have humbled me, my lady. I should like for you to help me, please. And with my own home. I should...I have a great deal of time that I have not used, and I think to be able to get away for a restripe would be great."

"Respite. And I do too. Sometimes just getting away for a few hours can rejuvenate you enough that you can feel like a new person." He left her then so that she could get his program set up. After about an hour, Arryn returned and she knew that something had happened. When he asked her to have a seat, Renie knew that it was bad.

"The demon has gone to Penny's home. We believe it was in search of the contract. Of course he didn't find it, but he was there all the same." Renie nodded. "Lord Damon wants to speed this up a bit. He wishes for you to call to the demon now so that he can finish this."

"But I have three days left." Arryn nodded. "I don't want to leave you. I love you. I can't...I need these three days with you and the others."

"And I love you. But he said that it is important to all that we do this now. He believes him to be making a contract now with another child. We might not be able to save him should we wait." Renie nodded and wrapped her arms around Arryn. "We will get through this, Renie.

And when we do, we'll be married and live a long and happy life together."

Renie didn't say anything, because she knew that this, like other things she'd hoped for, would be a puff of smoke before it was set. Things rarely worked out the way she wanted, and as much as she wanted this over with too, she didn't want it to end.

Chapter 9

The pieces of the protectors were in her hand. Jonas stared at them and had to wipe the saliva from his mouth several times as she continued to speak to him. He wanted to take her now, take her to his lair and count them out, but she was not his yet to take. Then he looked at her when she said something that caught his attention.

"You wish to do what?" When she repeated it, he just laughed. "I don't make bargains with the likes of you. Besides, what can you possibly have that I don't already own?"

"You think you have all of me when you have my soul, but there is a lot more to me than just that. For instance, I have a brain too." Jonas snorted. "What? You have no use for what I might know?"

"No. I don't. What you have between your thighs is all that I care about. And how well I'm going to fit deeply within your pussy. I will heat you in a way that no other has. And my cum will fill you daily until I tire of you. Which you should know will be less time than I first thought if you think to use that brain of yours. I don't even wish for you to ever speak when you are with me." She laughed at him and his temper flared. "You think I need you to speak? I don't. I want your mouth on my cock. Sucking me like you have no other. Do you know what it will do to you to have me fill you with all that I am?"

"Yeah, I have a pretty good idea. It will burn me from the inside out. As for you fucking me, there is more to life than just sex. Or do you not care about that?" He told her that he really didn't. "What about money? Do you have any use for it? I know how to get millions for you."

"Millions of dollars? You don't have that much money, do you? Your mother thinks you have a little, but not millions. You'd give it to me? That would be smart of you, but will not make a difference at all in how I treat you or fuck you." She huffed at him. "You wish to bargain with things that you cannot bring here with you when you come to me. Money, while a good thing, will not come when you come here."

"No. I can get other people's money. A lot of it. Why, just the other day, Boss asked me to change the money from the protectors to hard cash. I can skim a little...."

When she stopped talking, he stared at her. It looked to him as if she were thinking of something profoundly more important than he was saying to her. When Jonas said her name thrice she still did not look at him. It wasn't until he touched her that she looked at him. He knew that he'd hurt her, but she only stared at him.

"That's what they're doing." He had no idea what she was talking about and said so. "The bank...they're.... You know what? It doesn't matter. What was I saying?"

"You were saying that you could steal money for me and I would have millions." Nodding, she moved back from him when he started to reach for her again. That was when he saw what he'd done to her.

The imprint of his hand startled him. He'd never been able to mark anyone before, and was both pleased and terrified of it now. The other woman that he'd talked to just yesterday had screamed when he'd touched her, and now he had to wonder if he had marked her as well. Jonas wanted to end this pointless conversation now and go and see.

"Do we have a deal?" He told her that he didn't care. His mind was elsewhere right now and what she was saying was trivial. "So, you'll take me and only me tomorrow morning by coming to my apartment. Once you are there you'll let me have my computer to take with me, right?"

"Yes, yes. Whatever you need." Jonas tried to think if he'd touched Penny Sharp, and whether she had been marked as well. He was going to go there and mark her now if he could. Other demons would not be able to touch her should she decide to go over his head. The woman was still talking when he made his way back to his lair. He had things to do now and very little time to do it in.

The trip to Penny's home was quick. The woman was in bed with someone again and Jonas paused to watch. She was very creative in her sexual play and he had learned a few things from her in the last few weeks. Like this one.

There were two males in the bed with her today. The male beneath her was holding her onto his cock while she rode him. He'd seen women do that before. Pleasure bitches were very good at this kind of play too. But the man that stood in front of her, with his long dick in her mouth, was fucking her there as if it was her pussy. She was holding his balls in her hand tightly and he was pumping her hard. But the thing that had him freeing his own cock was how the man had a woman wrapped around his shoulders as she hung from the posts at the bed. He was eating her as if she were his last meal. He wanted a piece of this.

"Jonas." He heard his name but tried his best to ignore it. He was fisting quickly now and he was very close to coming. "Jonas, come to me now."

He found himself in the office of Lord Damon with his dick hard as stone and his balls full. Damon only turned his back on him while he adjusted himself back into his pants and tried not to think about how painful his cock was. He was going to go back there later and see if they were finished. That was the most enjoyable human sex he'd seen in a while.

"Your lordship. I was busy." Lord Damon said nothing but sat behind his desk. A chair appeared behind him, but he knew better than to sit without permission. Instead he stood there until he was told to have a seat.

"Do you know why I summoned you here today? And the next time I call to you, I don't care if your cock is squirting out all of your seed, you are to come to me immediately. But we will talk about your punishment on that later." Jonas only nodded. Soon now he'd be in charge and he'd have a few things to punish this man with. "Well?"

"Well, sire?" He tried to think what he had missed and then remembered. "Why you brought me here. I'm not sure, sire. I have been busy with our work. I sometimes think that I can do more, but I just don't know how. Perhaps you can tell me?"

"You have been busy, I will say that for you." Jonas was glad that someone had noticed. "But you tell me why you think I have brought you here when I have so much work to do already?"

"I'm not sure." When Peter appeared next to him, he nearly whimpered. He had been tortured and burned, and Jonas would bet anything the little shit had given him up too. He had a lot to say. "I don't know what this is about. What has Peter done that would concern me?"

"Don't you know?" Jonas looked away from Peter. It was sickening to see how someone had peeled his skin from his body; his face was not nearly as beautiful as Jonas's, but still it was a mess now. And his dick had been nearly burnt to the root. Someone had been using him as their plaything. "What do you think Peter told me when I asked him just an hour ago? What stories do you think he had to tell?"

Peter tried to speak but his lips no longer worked. His mouth was opening and closing, but Jonas noticed that his tongue was gone, as were most of his teeth. Jonas looked at Lord Damon and tried to think how he was going to save himself. He needed just a little more time and he'd have it all.

"You are struggling with a lie, no doubt." Before he could tell him that he wasn't, which was a lie too, Peter disappeared, but not before Jonas witnessed him burning more. "I have it on good authority that you are bringing a female here. One that you wish to keep for yourself."

Jonas looked at the empty seat where Peter had been and cursed the man under his breath. When Lord Damon laughed, Jonas looked at him. There was something on his face. Something that told Jonas that he'd best tread softly.

"I'm guessing that he didn't tell you the entire story." Lord Damon said nothing but continued to stare at him. He was thinking hard, so hard that his head hurt from it.

"Did he also tell you that this was his idea? That to bring her here was all his doing?"

"No, he did not. He said that you have had it in your head to have her here at all costs. And that you have reinforced your rooms so that no one would hear her screaming when you took her." Jonas made a decision right then not to trust anyone again. Not that he had trusted Peter all that much, but never again would he have anyone in his rooms. "Would you like to explain to me why, when I visited your rooms, I saw everything as he had said it would be?"

"Mayhap...maybe it was him that did this. To make it look as if I was guilty." Jonas tried to think if there was a way for him to come out on top. "I told him that you would be pissed about this. I even went so far as to tell him that Markum had done the same thing, and to remind him what had happened to him when he decided to bring a woman here."

"You did, did you?" Jonas nodded, on a roll now. But Lord Damon spoke before he could continue. "This woman? What is her name? What does she look like? Someone that I could fuck, perhaps?"

Jonas straightened up to tell him to stay the fuck away from her but he caught himself. To tell the lord of the realm to fuck himself might not go over as well as he'd first thought. Instead of speaking, Jonas took several deep breaths and let his mind work for him.

"She is a beauty, my lord. But her name eludes me for now." He had asked her several times what her name was, and she had skipped over it as if she knew what power it would hold. "Her hair is not just a dull color of the human's we see, but many. I know that it is not real, but it suits her well. With her tall and willow thin body, I think her able to take a good pounding and then roll over and take it in the ass as well. She will be a fantastic fuck."

Jonas reached down and adjusted his cock. It had been hard before, but now it was as if he had a fire in it, and he had a feeling that the woman would take good care of him. If he was to have her. And things were beginning to look like that might not happen.

"When does she come to me?" Again his temper flared up, but Jonas only nodded. "I should like to see this beauty that you will hand over to me the moment you have her."

"Her birthday, my lord. It is in nine days." A lie, but the demon wouldn't know it because he was sure that he'd never told Peter the exact date. "I have made a bargain with her to bring her here on her birthday. And I will take her to you as soon as she arrives."

"See that you do." Jonas nodded and stared to rise, but Lord Damon spoke again. "What of this bargain that you've made with her? Tell me the details."

Damn it. He'd let that part slip. He should remember who he was talking to, as nothing seemed to get by him. As he tried to think of a good bargain, he also thought of the woman. Christ, she was going to have to be killed before the time to take her to Lord Damon. Because once she was there, he'd get everything from her and he'd be as good as fucked, like Markum was.

"Bargain. The bargain that I have with her says that she is tired of the life she is living." It was a stupid answer and Lord Damon cocked a brow at him. "What I mean is, she has asked for a power. A power over the device that can move money. She wishes to make herself rich so that she can enjoy her last days on the other realm."

"A computer." Jonas nodded and smiled. "And these monies that she wants. I suppose she'd want to share them with me as well. I like that plan. There are a few things in the other realm that I can use here. But we cannot steal them, as you might know."

"You'll take my money…her money as well?" Jonas realized what he'd said and that he was towering over the desk. Sitting back down he tried to regain some control over his temper, but it was difficult. "I mean your money, of course. And you should have it. There are many things that could be used here that you could provide for us. I forget myself at times."

"You are angry. I don't understand why this emotion is there when you know that I should have more than you." Jonas wanted to deny it but nodded. "You don't think I should have it all, Jonas? You don't think that as your lord that I should have first pick of the woman? That I should not be able to fuck her pretty pussy before you? I am a man who likes a tight hole to fuck, and you think to deny me that?"

"No, my lord. I do not…I have seen her from afar and have a yearning to fuck her as well." A pleasure bitch appeared before him, and he looked at her body before speaking again. "While she is a nice way to relieve the pressure, she is not the human."

"Nay, she is not. But you will fuck her. Now. Here on my desk." Jonas watched as the bitch moved to the large desk and lay back on it. Then as she stroked her cock while her other hand played with her clit, Jonas felt his own cock shrivel and his balls tighten to his body. "I should like to see you suck her off too, Jonas. I would not like to take all your pleasure away."

"Sire?" The man roared out his displeasure and Jonas stood up. He was going to have to do this and there was nothing he could do about it. Moving to the woman, he leaned down to take her into his mouth when he was grabbed from behind. His head was shoved at her cock so quickly that Jonas couldn't help but gag.

It wasn't that he didn't care for sex, with anyone for that matter, but he wanted the human. And nothing else was going to do. As his head was physically moved up and down over her extra appendage, he thought of the woman. His cock hardened just a little and he reached down to stroke himself. But before he could get any harder, a hand was wrapped around his and jerked from his cock. The pain of it had him wanting to check to see if his cock had been ripped from his body.

"You will seek your pleasure, Jonas, when I say you can." He wanted to scream. Jonas wanted to tell him that he was going to kill him. Tell the lord that in no time, he'd be the one in charge and his life was going to be hell. But he didn't. Not yet. He had to wait, and the waiting would be so much sweeter because of this.

When the bitch came, he wiped his mouth with his robe as he was told to do and spit as much of her caustic cum out of his mouth as he could manage. It was burning now, his throat on fire from it, but he knew that it would heal soon enough. But before he could leave to do that, Lord Damon told him to have a seat.

"When this woman of mine comes here, I want to be informed. In fact, when you leave to get her, I will come with you. I should like to see the other world again." Jonas started to speak but Lord Damon raised a brow at him. "You have some objections, Jonas?"

"It's just that she might be frightened enough as it is." He nodded at him and Jonas was relieved. "I shall let you know when I go to get her and when I return. That way she can become used to her surroundings."

"You have my needs, Jonas. You will let me go with you." When Lord Damon stood, so did Jonas. "That is all. And if you go against me, what Markum is going through will not even be close to what I do to you. I have come up with some very delightful ways to make you suffer. And suffer you will. For you have thwarted me enough on matters of the other realm."

As soon as he was in his room, Jonas started screaming out his frustrations. He threw his things—some he treasured, some he did not—around the room until they were in broken pieces at his feet. Clothing was torn to shreds. His mirror was broken and sent flying. Even his bed was destroyed as he let his frustrations out. When he was spent, he sat down. It was time to plan what to do about Lord Damon.

"He will not know the meaning of the suffering I shall put upon his body. And I will spit in his face when he cries out his pain." Jonas sat back against the wall and smiled. "The king himself will say that I've done a good job on this, for he himself will not recognize his right hand man when I have finished with him."

~~~

Arryn watched Renie work. She was onto something, she'd said to him earlier, and he was amazed at the amount of energy she was giving it. Tracking it down, she'd told him; she was tracking it down to find the man who would do this. And no matter what he said, she never heard him.

The bank, it was discovered, was not involved in the theft as she'd thought. Not at the local level, anyway. There was something about addresses that couldn't be accounted for, as well as a few places that had been bounced from more than once. Arryn had no idea what she meant by that, but it was fun to see her explaining it to him as if he should. When Dan appeared in the room with them, he moved to go and talk to him.

"The pantry is finished, as are the cabinets in the kitchen. I like what you wanted, and would like to use it again if you would not mind." Arryn told him that it was fine with him, but it was Renie's idea. "I can see the use of the chalk board and metal fronts on cabinets in the bathroom as well. Leaving notes when necessary, hanging up some of your information you need to see when shaving. Brilliant. And the lighting that you had me put in all the rooms is natural, as well as clean and bright."

"She said that she likes to cook. I don't think she believes, however, that she will be here to do any. I think her mouth says what we want to hear, but her heart is thinking she will die on the morrow." Dan looked at her when Arryn did. She was deep into her work. "Finishing this project is her priority for the moment. She told me yesterday that she was very close to getting the answer for Dusty and the others."

"I've spoken to Judith and Kala as well. I had no idea that so much money was being taken, or that all the accounts we have opened are having the same issues." Arryn was surprised by that as well. Millions of dollars were taken from the eleven accounts that had been opened recently by the other protectors, as well as the monies set aside for the shelter and other projects. "Do you think she will be able to get it all back?"

"She said that she will. It is only a matter of chasing down the culprit. I think about an hour ago she actually found the money. I have never seen a person so frustrated by finding something they were seeking before." Dan nodded and smiled at him. "She is a sight when she is frustrated. I was just thinking of ways that I could...well, never mind. I will speak to her about this idea I have."

It had been almost funny. She had cursed a streak of words that made him think to write a few of them down. Two he was still looking for some information on, and the rest...well, they were ones that he'd never use, of course, but they were quite colorful. Dan told him that he was going to start on the floor now and wondered if they had decided on what they wanted. Arryn retrieved the block of wood that he and Renie had decided on before coming down from their room that morning.

The dining room would have hard wood floors. He had wanted it to be dark, like the walls in their room, but she said that light would be better. It would be friendlier when they entertained, and much easier to keep clean. He really didn't understand that part since they had a housekeeper, but it was what she wanted and he was in agreement as well.

When he sat back down across from her, he was set to start on his crossword puzzle again. It was amazing to him that a small computer could have so much entertainment value for him. There were more crosswords on this device than he'd seen in a very long time. When he picked it up, he glanced at Renie and noticed that she was staring at him, not through him as she'd been doing all day.

"It's going to be easier now." He nodded. "I have to make some notes here and then I want to drop this off at

Kala's house. Do you want to come with me? I want to see the babies again."

"I would like that." Arryn stretched out his legs. "You're going to say goodbye to them, aren't you? I want you to know that I no longer think it's necessary for you to say goodbye to everyone. We are going to win out on this, and we'll live a long and very happy life. Even when I upset you, I think you to be happy."

Instead of answering him, she turned back to her computer. His heart broke for her and he didn't know how to tell her that she was going to be fine. Just last night, before they'd gone to bed, she'd told him a few things that had happened to her that made her disbelieve what was going to happen.

"My mother never liked me. Never. I don't know what it was about me that made me realize that from the start, but she didn't. For days on end she'd just do what was necessary to keep children's services off her back. I guess the neighbors had turned her in once before. But by the time I was three or four, I knew that she hated me." When he pulled Renie into his arms, she continued her story as if she was telling him the weather. It was cold and without emotion. But he knew inside that she was hurting more than she would ever say.

"We were at the grocery store. I had...I guess like most kids, I wanted to have something special for my birthday. Penny told me that I wasn't worth the cost of the plastic it would cost the store to wrap up a cake for me, and I should get the notion out of my head that she was going to buy me a thing." Arryn wanted to find Penny Sharp and show her what she'd done to her daughter's bleeding heart. Before he could tell her how sorry he was, Renie continued. "I was looking at the cakes in the display cakes, not saying a word, when a woman came up behind me and asked me which one I liked the most. I had my heart set on the one with the big blue flowers on it. Chocolate, with buttercream frosting, too. I didn't tell her that I also wanted my name on it, with hearts all around it. That would have been just too much to think about after...after Penny had told the store that not only was I not worthy of the cake but also that I was a liar and a thief. But the woman told the employee to box it up."

"She bought it for you." Renie had nodded and that was when he felt the first of many tears burn into his chest. "Was it as good as you thought it would be?"

"I never got to eat it. As soon as the woman gave Penny the cake, she put it in the trunk of the car and slammed the lid closed. I thanked the woman, told her how much I appreciated it, but Penny just jerked me along and shoved me in the car too. All the way home, she never said a single word to me." Arryn let Renie go when she stood up and went to the long window. The moon shone in on her, silhouetting her figure for him to see. "The cake was the last thing she brought in that day. It was laid on the table and the plastic was taken off. She searched around for some candles. I had no idea that we'd even had any, but she unearthed five of them. As she lit them, using her cigarette to do so, I thought of how much I was going to enjoy my first cake."

Arryn knew that whatever had happened after that was going to be bad. He knew that Renie had not only not gotten any of the cake, but something had been done to her that she'd never asked for it again. He would bet, with all his life, that Penny had done something so horrific to her daughter that day that it had stayed with her for the rest of her life. And he was sure he didn't want to know what it was.

"Plates were bought out. The candles sputtered and burned while she fussed with the table cloth, something we never used. Then just as she sat down to cut into it, she asked me to make a wish and blow out the candles. I was leaning forward to do just that when she hit me; doubled her fist and hit me in the face. As I tumbled back, she picked up the cake, still with the burning candles, and threw it on me. My dress, the one that I'd found in the garbage the week before, burned my skin before I could get it out."

He'd gotten up and held her then, sat on the window seat and held her while she sobbed. Arryn talked to her, never really sure what he said, but he knew that it was all he could do, because the alternative was to find Penny Sharp and harm her...hurt her for all the pain she'd caused such a wonderful, loving person.

Arryn held her long after he'd put her to bed and she'd fallen asleep. Thinking of all the things he was going to do for her, he reached for Kala. After he told her what Renie had told him, Kala decided that she wanted to plan a party for the woman, and give her the best birthday that anyone could ever have. Arryn thought it a wonderful idea, but asked her to do it the day after the thing with the demon was over.

"We can celebrate it then without having this pall hanging over us." Kala agreed and asked him to describe the cake for her. He gave her as much detail as he could find in her memories, and told her of one more thing he'd found there. This really was going to be a grand party.

Chapter 10

Today. Today she was going to hell. As Renie went over her notes again for Riss, she thought of this morning. Arryn had been so tender to her at first that she'd cried after he made the sweetest and most gentle love to her. As she sat there she thought of it again, of how he'd taken her hard enough that she was still sore even hours later.

"I love the way you moan when I touch you." She had moaned, a great deal as a matter of fact. His hands could do things to her body that defied description. "Your skin is so soft, smooth. I could touch you all the time and never get enough."

He had her on her belly and he sat on her thighs. Arryn was digging deep into the muscles of her ass so hard that she knew that she'd be bruised the next day and not even care. As he moved over her thighs, then down to her knees, every part of her body seemed to melt under his administrations. When he lifted her leg up and bit into her calf, she nearly came and begged him to do it again.

"Not yet, love. I have so much more of you to explore, and if you finish now, whatever will I do?" She'd been too overwhelmed to answer him, but his soft chuckle had her wanting to turn over and show him what she could do with her own toys. But the sound of her vibrator turning on made her look over her shoulder at him. "You can come with this device. I've seen it used before, but I've never had the pleasure of using one."

"Are you going to use it on you?" He nodded, then ran it over her ass. It was too much and not enough at the same time. "Make me come, Arryn, please. I need to come."

"In due time." He moved down her legs with the vibrator, then up over her ass again. She was so wet by then that she knew that the bed was going to be soaked. As her legs were spread open, she tried to fight the urge to beg him again, and that was when he nipped at her ass.

Renie thought for sure that he was going to kill her. Every time she was close to coming, he moved his mouth and the vibrator to another sensitive part of her body. By the time he had told her to move to her back, she was a bundle of tense nerves. A cool breeze, she had thought, would have sent her over the edge, and she was suddenly craving a big fan.

He held the vibrator to his cock, stroking the length of it as he held it in his other fist. Renie sat up, watching his face for moments and then his hands on his cock. There was so much precum leaking from him that she felt her mouth water at the thought of tasting him. Moving to the foot of the bed where he was, Renie took him into her mouth just as he pressed the vibrator to her pussy.

She was sure that the entire house had heard her. Her scream of release—and that was just what it was—had felt like she'd been set on a rocket and it had blown her up. Even as she was coming back to earth, her body came again...not just her, but her entire being seemed to have been put on a ride of coming that was never going to end. And as soon as Arryn came, his cum hitting the back of her throat with enough force that she was surprised that her head wasn't thrown back, Renie came again and again. But he hadn't been finished. No, not yet.

He threw her back on the bed, she with her legs wide and his cock buried into her, even as she reached for him. Arryn slammed deep, and Renie's body bent nearly double with her legs up and over his shoulders. The odd position didn't take away from her pleasure. Even as he squeezed her breasts, bit them hard, she cried out her release. And when he came too, filling her with his seed, Renie felt the earth move beneath them, the bed trembling in response as he threw back his head and cried out how much he loved her.

"Renie?" It took her several seconds to focus on the man in front of her and she moved back in fear. "It's me, Riss. You called for me to come here."

Her heart was pounding as she tried to think. But he never moved, never came any closer than the doorway as she tried her best not to let her fear take over. *It's today*, her mind kept saying in a loop. Today she was going to die.

"Renie? I'm not going to hurt you." She nodded, not really sure of anything right now other than she had been scared. "I'm going to come closer to you so that I can touch you. All right?"

"I'm...it's okay. Just give me a minute." Riss nodded and moved into the room with her. He never touched her like he had said, but she did put out her hand to him. "I'm not sure if it will burn you, but I would like the contact please."

His fingers brushed gently over her hand, then he took it into his. There was no heat this time...warmth, but nothing like when she'd touched Boss or Lily. His arms wrapped around her as she stood up, and Renie let his comfort wash over her. When he finally let her go, he held her hand while he sat at the table with her. It was as if she'd been bathed in his comfort and love. Looking at him, she gave him a half smile and shook her head.

"You must think I'm a dork." He told her that he had no idea what that could be, but he was sure she wasn't anything like that. "I'm scared, if you want to know the truth. I wonder...I keep wondering if I'll be lit on fire, or will he just take me there like I am right now."

"He is to meet you here, I thought." Renie nodded. "There will be no taking you, Renie. You know that we have your ribs."

"Back. You have my back." He nodded and smiled at her. "Why is it that Arryn seems to be more...I don't know...up on things, I guess? Most of the rest of you seem to be stuck forever in the dark ages. Well, not quite that far back, but you know what I mean. And Michael? He is positively adorable the way he messes up nearly every word."

"Arryn's interaction with humans is legendary. One time, during a war between some of the states, he was found beside some of the other protectors fighting as if he were human too. I am not sure how long he had been there before it was discovered, but he said that he learned a great deal during that time. He told me later that he never fired his gun, but it was a learning experience that he would never forget, and that the food served was as bad as anything he'd tried to cook for himself." Renie laughed, as she was sure Riss had meant for her to. "It has been that way for so many years. On his time off he would work the counter at fast food restaurants, or in a clothing store. He knows money, too; not as well as you do, but he has a better understanding of it than I do. And you should see his closet. There are so many shirts that he was required to wear on these jobs that it is amazing to me that he has not had to have a bigger storage place put in just for them. When I think on it, I don't believe I've ever seen him wear them other than to work. You think he keeps them as something he treasures?"

"I think you're right about the shirts. He showed them to me after he moved them to our home. And they are in a separate closet from the one in our room. It's filled with jeans and tee shirts now. But the rest of you? I've noticed that…what's up with Valyn? I mean, he doesn't even seem to like us…human's, I mean." Riss nodded, then looked away. "You don't have to tell me. I know that whatever it is, it must have been terrible for him."

"It was. And while I know of the story and what transpired that year, I do not have all the details. Valyn took some time off after that. A decade or more. I thought him never to return."

"But he has. And I think the scars are still there. Has it been…how long ago was this?" Riss looked like he wasn't going to answer, but when he did, Renie felt something move in her heart. "So long ago. Two hundred years is a long time to hold so much pain in your heart."

"I agree. And I hope…I am not sure, but I do hope that Boss has a bride for him. She will need to be strong, much stronger than even you and my Kala. She will need to be something more than…it will be a hard boat for her to row."

Riss asked her what it was she wanted and she opened the file in front of her before speaking. "This is the address that is moving the money. It's not a physical address but one that the computer has. I think it's the bank manager, but I'm not a hundred percent sure at the moment. Do you understand IP addresses?"

"I have some knowledge of them. You have narrowed it down then? Will the others be able to get their money returned to them?" She nodded and smiled. "I do not think that is a smile that I should like turned on me. What is it you have done?"

"The day after tomorrow the money will be returned to all the accounts. Some of it has been moved, but not a lot of it. I think this person thinks that he's much smarter than me. But he's not. There is another person helping him. A nephew, I think. I know of him, but I have never met him personally. His skills are good, but not...I've called in a few favors, and he'll be arrested while this is going down with the bank." Riss asked her if she knew it was a man. "No, not really, but a woman would be more precise in her taking it, I think. She'd have a better system set up. I have no idea why I think that, but there you have it. Also—and this is way out there—I think a woman would have been more inclined to stop at a certain point. So as not to get caught. Not to say that there aren't more than a few greedy women out there, but this just feels like a man's job."

"But why are you handing this off to me? Or the group, as you will be able to do this on your own?" Renie handed him another file. It was the real reason she'd invited him there. "What is this?"

"It's my will. I had it drawn up last week. And if you would be so kind to have my wishes taken care of, I'd be very grateful." Riss looked it over, and she knew when he got to the part where she distributed out her funds. "I've been paid well over the years. And I'm pretty good at investments too. Very good. My last several jobs paid me so well that had I wanted to I could have retired on the funds. But I got bored just sitting around, and that was what landed my butt in jail. I think knowing that my…that Penny had done this to me was more than my heart and mind could take at the time."

"Understandable. But you know that you will not need this. We will be there for you, every step of the way." She pushed the file back at him when he started to hand it back. "You're not going to be his plaything."

"And if something happens, then this will be taken care of. Penny will come after you, I'm sure. When she does, you'll find a letter there for her. Not that it will help her understand what I've done, but it did ease my heart some." He nodded and took the file. "And the other things? You'll take care of them as well?"

"Yes." Nodding, she sat back down at the computer. "Renie, can you tell me why your mother did this to you?"

"I believe…no, that's not right. I know that she hated me. And she hated everyone along with it. I'm sure if someone were to ask her she'd tell them that she did the best she could for me. You know, sending me away when I turned six. But she didn't send me so much as I ran. And every time I ran and I was brought back, I would get further and further away from her. Until one day, I just never returned." She looked at Riss, one of the nicest men she knew. "She did this to me because she felt that she deserved it. That her life was forever changed because someone had planted me in her belly. Does that make sense?"

"Yes. In a sad sort of way, it does." Nodding, he turned to the door as if to leave, then stopped before speaking again. "The protectors are all here that could be.

All of them have you in their prayers today. And you'll see that we really do have your back in all of this."

Renie got up when he opened the door wider. As they made their way to the front of the house, she could feel it. And when he opened the outside door for her and she stepped onto the porch, it was to see a sight that she would bet her very life on that no one had ever seen before. Protectors—hundreds, maybe thousands of them—standing in Arryn's yard with their wings spread and their swords drawn. They had come to save her. She could only nod at them as the tears fell down her cheeks, and each of them bowed before her with their swords to their forehead.

~~~

Damon watched the little pisser as he snuck by the doors. Jonas thought that he could do this and no one would be the wiser. Well, he was wrong about that, almost dead wrong. And only because he wasn't going to die. Not today anyway, and more than likely not for many, many years to come.

When a heavy hand landed on his shoulder, Damon did not have to turn to see who it was. He knew. The man behind him would make others tremble in their boots, wet their pants, and then die where they stood. The king of this world had come to see the sight, he was sure. Damon had told him everything that was going to happen today.

"I should like to be there, but not where anyone can see me." Damon nodded and bowed lower when his king stood in front of him. "This demon, does he have a clue what is going to happen to him? What will befall him once he tries to take this woman from her family?"

"I think he believes himself to be above such punishment. He even lied to me when his cohort was there beside him. Jonas will suffer greatly for his actions. And I only wish I could be the one serving it to him." The king nodded as he told Damon to stand up. "Sire, should you go, the other king will need to know you are there. You know how he is on rules."

"I have spoken to him." Of course he had. Damon should have known that they would have spoken. "The woman, the one that signed the contract, she is to come here. Now."

When the woman appeared before him, Damon looked at her with the eye of one who knew evil, and this woman was more evil than any human he'd seen brought there before. When she asked why she was there, no one answered her. Damon wasn't sure either, but he would never question his king.

"I asked you a question. Are you so stupefied by my looks that you are not able to speak? If not, then why the hell am I here?" Damon was sure that was not what she had meant, but said nothing as she repeated her demand for answers. She dared gaze at his king, and then she smiled at him. "I've been brought here to see her, haven't I? I mean, today is the big day, isn't it? It might be tomorrow or the next day, but I know it is soon. I want to see the party going on with my daughter."

"You know not when your child was born to you?" She looked at him, then at his king when he spoke again. "You have not a clue what the date is, do you? Her birth is not for another day and a half. But today, as you have put it, it is the day of her celebration."

She was offered a chair and a drink. Pleasure bitches, unused to seeing a human in their midst, were obviously curious about her and touched her whenever they could get close enough as they brought her everything they could think of. Even a tray of stones, hot from the fire, was set on the table next to her. Damon had a thought that the woman might have already been inducted into their realm, as there were no burns on her body after being touched. When he looked at his king, he only nodded but said nothing more. So the woman was theirs. He wondered how long it would be before she understood what was going to happen.

"When do you leave?" Damon told the king that he was just getting ready. "Then what should we wear? I am to understand that there is a protocol about such things. Not to look like an elf, I'm to understand. I wish I had been there to see that. Someday you will have to dress so that I might have the same pleasure as they had."

Damon flushed. He would never live that one down and only smiled at the king. When he shook his big body the changes in him were immediate, as they were in the king too. They stood together, looking to all the other realms like two men having lunch. Even Jonas would never recognize them once they were there.

As soon as they arrived at the small deli, a young man—Kipling, they knew him by—seated them. He, too, was clueless as to who they were, and Damon thought it a good thing. The rest of the room, all of them protectors hidden in the shadows, knew just who they were and watched them with their swords drawn but at ease. For now.

"She is loved." Damon had figured that out when he'd been there two days earlier. He had been warned, several times, that should anything go wrong in this, everyone would pay and dearly. The man they called Boss was very upset with how long this had been going on. "I should like to speak to her when this is finished. Just to meet the person who would have so many at her call to arms."

Damon didn't know if that was a good idea or not, but would ask. Before Damon could say that he would arrange it if he could, the woman walked in, and beside her was her mate, a man that Damon knew to be of good standing.

He might not have the same beliefs as the men who served Boss, but he did respect a man who was loyal to his king. Arryn, along with the other men who were with him, was said to be a good man, a great one by many. Arryn the Avenger was hailed by all who knew him. Damon knew that should it come to it, he would gladly give his life for the woman, and she him.

"You have brought what I asked for? The things that are in the contract?" Jonas moved from the wall where he'd been hiding and toward the girl. Damon realized then that not only had he not seen the others in the room, but he could not feel them either. A glance at the king made him realize how much he and Boss had spoken. Jonas thought himself alone with the girl.

"I have. And you'll get them when you answer a few questions for me." Jonas snorted and told her that he was in charge. "No, you're not. For the moment, I am. Now. I'd like to know why you lied about your name on the contract."

"My name? You have no idea whether or not I have lied on anything." Reyna only stood there staring at him. "You do know where I hail from, do you not? It is within my rights to lie about everything. So what. Hand over the pieces and let us be on our way."

"I don't have them on me." Damon was surprised by that, but when he started to stand—to do what, he had no idea—his king stopped him with a hand on his. He sat back down, but was watchful of what was going to happen next. "You want them, then you'll do as I want for a change. Understood?"

"You have no rights at all, girl. And should you think that, I'll burn them from you the moment I get between your legs. Do you have any idea how hot my cock is going to be inside of you? How much I'm going to enjoy burning your flesh from you?" Jonas laughed, but it was slightly forced and Damon wondered about that. "And when I am done with you, had my fill, I plan to sell you to the highest bidder and watch while they fuck you as well."

"You think so?" Jonas nodded. "I don't. I mean, I guess you can take me with you, provided that everything is in order on the contract, but I'm not going to have sex with you. You're a liar and a cheat. I don't have sex with men that do that."

"You believe yourself to have a choice in this matter?" Reyna nodded and smiled. "You have nothing. Less than nothing. Come with me now, I tire of it here."

"Too bad." Reyna sat down and Jonas looked ready to have a fit. "We're going to go over this line by line so I can make sure that I'm not being...well, fucked over by you."

"I said now." His king stood the moment Jonas reached for her, and as Jonas put his hands on the girl, the king put his on Jonas. The look on his face was comical. And then he turned to look around the room. "What is the meaning of this?"

"Meaning? I shall show you the meaning." Their king shook his body and morphed into his natural state. "Do you understand the meaning now, Robert Lenny? Or do you go by James Fitzpatrick? Perhaps you might go by your given name, the one your mother spit upon you when you were brought from the split in her thighs, Arnold Malone. "

Jonas dropped to the floor, his wings, dark and sooty, spread out over him even as Reyna stood up. When she started to back away from them, Arryn was suddenly behind her and held her still as he whispered into her ear. Damon had but a moment to wonder what he might be saying to her when Jonas…Arnold spoke.

"I was bringing her to you, my lord." The king only laughed. "I was, my lord. This I swear. Lord Damon wanted her for himself, but I told him that she was for you and only you. But he said that it mattered nothing to him what you wanted. He said he was in charge and you were nothing to him."

"Did he now? What have you to say about this, Lord Damon?" Damon shook his body and changed to himself too. When he towered over the man they all knew as Jonas, he leaned over and picked him up by his throat. "He says that you were to take this morsel from me. Is that true?"

"Nay, my lord. You know that it is not." They both looked at Reyna when she stood before them. "What have you to say, Lady Reyna? You wish to beg for his life?"

"No, and hell no. I only want to know what is to happen now. I mean, I should be allowed to know where I stand in all this." She looked at Arnold then back at Damon. "I don't want to come with you. I mean, you might be a really nice person—I doubt it, but you never know…I'm babbling. I don't want to go. Can you tell me what…where do I stand, please?"

"You are free." Arnold disappeared and the two of them, his king and himself, were joined by Boss and Michael. Each of them had a great deal to lose should a fight start, and Damon had a feeling that it was closer to happening then anyone had realized. "If you would be so kind as to call your men to stand down, my lady, I will tell you everything."

"My men?" He nodded when she looked at him. Bewilderment was evident all over her face. "These people are my friends. I mean, I don't know all of them, but they came when I needed them, and for that I will call them friends. But they aren't my men."

"As you wish." The king sat and so did the rest of them. The only one standing was Reyna, and she looked very confused. "The contract is void. Not for just the name that is signed across the bottom, but the fact that you are no longer a single unit. Also, your lord here believes that Arnold planned the entire conception. He is there, just in the shadows, when the rape occurred. I will find out. You will not, but I will find out."

"So I never had a chance from the moment that I was conceived, did I?" No one said a word. "What do you mean about the contract? I don't understand. You mean because I'm in love with Arryn it voided the contract between us?" The king shook his head and said that it was more than that. "Then perhaps you can tell me. Because I'd really like some good news today."

"The contract states that he will take you and only you on your twenty-fifth birthday. When you spoke to Arnold, you said those words to him, just as you were told to do by Lord Damon. Only on that date and only you." She still didn't get it, and Damon wanted to laugh. But the king was not finished explaining just yet. "And even though your date of birth is still a day away, there would have been no way for him to have been able to take you. You are no longer alone."

"You keep saying that. And if you think that helps clear it up, then you're nuttier than he was." Damon stood up and ten of the protectors stood as well. Reyna looked at the men behind her and asked them to wait. Damon sat back down, but he looked ready to attack if need be. "I'm sure that the next words out of his mouth will explain it all before I have to impale him on a blade myself."

"You are no longer alone because you carry a child that cannot be taken to my realm." The king stood up and so did Damon. But when Renie sat down, there were two people helping her to press her head between her knees. "You will do well, my lady. And you are free from any hold that my realm had on you."

"And the others?" The king looked at him and Damon nodded as Reyna continued. "I know there are at least two more woman who have done this. What happens to their children? Are you just going to do this for me?"

"I will…." The king looked at Boss. "I will look into this, you have my word. And any children, what shall I do with them? I have no need for souls that are given this way."

"You bring them to me and I will make sure that they are cared for." The king nodded and they turned to go. But he looked back at Reyna, then her mate.

"I have a gift for you. I am not a man who bestows gifts, so I would very much like for you to consider taking this." Arryn looked at his own king before nodding. "Thank you."

The touch was light, the mark small. Damon knew what it was the moment that he saw it. He had just granted the man access to the king of hell.

As soon as they both were in the king's office, Arnold was brought to them. The man was still spilling lies even as he was read his punishment. And Damon thought that he'd enjoy this much more than he ever did playing with Markum.

Chapter 11

"I don't understand." Arryn didn't really either but told her that he loved her. "I love you too, but I still don't understand what just happened. Do you?"

"No. I'm not sure…maybe Boss knows." But when he looked for the man, he was gone. "I'll see if I can find him for you."

"No. Don't leave me just yet." He didn't want to leave her and picked her up and put her on his lap. "What did he mean about a baby, Arryn? I think that was the part that has me the most confused. Do you think he was having fun with us? To be honest, I wouldn't have thought he had a sense of humor, but I have been wrong before."

"I can't father a child." Or so he had thought. "Damon told me once that I was nearly human when I was with you. I assumed that he thought that I acted like one. I was quite proud of that."

"So you think it's possible? That somehow you and I are going to have a baby?" When she stiffened in his arms, he nearly let his wings go before she spoke. "I can't have four babies at once, Arryn. I love you and all, but having four at one time is just more than I think I can handle. I can barely pick up after myself. Four babies and working with the Mystics? I just don't think…I'll love them and you, but it's going to be something…it's going to be hard, but we can do it."

Michael appeared before them and Arryn noticed that he was smiling. It was sort of a scary thing to see on his face, as Michael was not known for his sense of humor. Not that he didn't have one, but he wasn't very demonstrative of it. Nor did the man usually get the most common of jokes.

"He should like to see you both now. It is time." Renie asked time for what. "To be married, of course."

"No." They both looked at Renie as if she wasn't serious. "I'm not going to marry Arryn because I find myself suddenly knocked up. And I'm pretty sure I am, aren't I?"

"Knocked up?" Arryn explained the term to Michael. "You are with child, yes. So you must marry. It is time. Come along now."

Renie sat down, and Arryn might have laughed but he was sort of afraid of her. She looked…well, determined came to mind. Michael looked at him as if he had some say over her.

"She said no. And I'm pretty sure that she means it." Michael huffed. "I don't know what to tell you, buddy. But I don't think she's going to come with you. And if she won't, then I won't either."

"You have been summoned." Neither of them looked to be going anywhere, so Arryn sat down as Michael started to pace. "When you are summoned, you are to come with me. Or to show up on your own. Is that what you have planned? That you are coming on your own free bill?"

"Free will, and no. I'm not coming at all. I'm not going to be one of those brides that has people counting on one hand the date of their marriage to the birth of their child." Arryn explained this to Michael as well. "You need to get out more. And while I'm sorry that you're put between a rock and a hard place...where you are in the middle of this, but I'm not going to do it. Not now at any rate. The next thing you'll be telling me is that I'm going to have to learn to fly and will live for a long time."

"Forever, as a matter of fact. And you do have wings. Since the moment that you were freed of this contract. But that does not make it so you can ignore a summons. You will be...come with me, please." When Renie looked at Arryn, he nodded.

"Yes, you have wings. I noticed when you were on my lap. As for you being an immortal, that too is something that came to me when I touched you. Much the same as it has come to the other protectors. They will no longer need to protect you as they have before. You are like us." Arryn watched her face for any sign that she was going to freak out. But she looked at Michael and smiled.

"Do I have a sword too?" Michael nodded and backed from her. "Tell me, Michael, honey, how do I call it to use?"

"I do not think it would be wise of me to explain such a thing to you. You look positively mad with your need to cause harm." Renie stood up and Michael backed up more. "Lady Reyna, you will do well to remember that I am the right hand person to Boss. He needs me."

"Not as much as I need to hurt you right now." When Michael disappeared, Renie turned to Arryn. "That was mean, I know, but it was fun. But we do have to talk."

"I love you." Renie said that she loved him as well, but he watched her. She no more knew what she was saying than he did when he was upset. "Perhaps if we went to talk to Boss he could explain things to us."

"He's tricky." Boss was, Arryn knew that. "Once we step into His office we'll be as good as wed. Where is His office, anyway?"

Arryn told her. "He has one here as well, but I've no idea where it might be. For all I know it could be at the compound."

She continued to pace and speak just under her breath. Arryn let her; it was the way she worked things out, and this was something that she'd have to work through on her own. Reaching for Boss, Arryn told Him what was going on. His laugher made him smile.

Michael is beside himself with concern. He seems to think that my only course of action is to go there and demand that she listen to him. I told him that she might hurt us. I think he believes she would cause us dire harm. Boss laughed again but continued. *She is concerned for the babe? And there is only the one this time. I know that you have been worried about that as well.*

She was. He watched her pace, thinking it was the most beautiful sight he'd ever seen. *I am in love with her and can wait her out should she need this.*

You are not worried that she will change her mind then? Arryn told Him that she looked to be set in her ways about this. *That's all right, for now. I should like to see her, however. There are a few things that I must explain to you both about the mark you were given.*

Arryn looked down at the scar on his wrist and wondered why the king had done such a thing. *Then Renie is marked as well, like I have been?*

You both are, as will your children be marked. I can tell you some, but I'd rather tell you both. He told Him what Renie said about Him being tricky. His laughter boomed across their connection. *I am at that. But I will not do anything that she does not wish. As for you being wed, in all eyes you are anyway. I need only to set the bond with the rings I have made for you both.*

I'll let her know when she calms a bit more. She will be happy to know that we are to have only one child. Boss said He'd like to talk to him about that as well. *The other children, you mean?*

I do. There are only the two of them. One is nearly ten, the other is but five. Both of them are boys and have been...let me just say that had they been in my care from the beginning, they would have been better nourished. And not just with food either. They are sorely lacking in any kind of affection or love.

We'll talk to You soon. I promise You. She is beginning to wind down now, so I won't think it to be much longer. I heard from Judith and Kala that Dusty has the party all ready to go. You think you'll be there on time? Boss laughed again and Arryn thought that he could go his entire life just to hear Him do that more often. *You are happy, aren't you? I don't mean about the baby and that we've got another Mystic; but in general, You're happy.*

I am. And I shall be. We will have a grand time and I will have too much cake, along with that punch that Dusty makes. Kipling says it's the only thing she can make and she does it very well. Also, the gift is there too, the new car you have gotten for her. What a thing to give someone for their birthday. And such an odd shade of green. I should like to share something with you that I have with no one else, not even Michael as yet. When you meet up with Tholan's wife — and there will be one — you will think me quite mad. He asked Him why. *You shall have to wait. I should like to bring her along now, but there is*

Valyn to care for. Yes, he is next in my Mystics, but he will…it is needed for him now.

I will talk to her, then we will come to see You. We will need to take care of a few things at our home if we're to take on a couple more children. Ten and five are good ages. I cannot wait to meet them. Boss told him soon. Very soon, should Renie agree. *I'll have a talk with her now. Perhaps it will change her mind about killing Michael if she has something else to focus on.*

Doubtful, but one can hope. When the connection was closed, he could still feel the humor coming from his friend…and He was his friend, as well as his boss. When Renie sat across from him, he told her again how much he loved her.

"What did He say?" He asked her who. "You know who. I'm guessing that Michael told Him that I was being pig headed about this, and now He's demanding that we get married. I'm not going to be forced."

"He is disappointed, but not upset. He wanted to talk to me about the other children. Two boys. I think He'd like for us to raise them with our own child. I told him it would be up to you." She stood up again, went to the window this time, and stared out. He wished they were at their home and felt the air around them shift. Renie turned to look at him with a raised brow.

"Did you bring me here so that no one could hear me yelling?" He simply told her that he wanted to be home, with her. "These boys, how old are they and what…just so you know, we will take them if you want. I do, but we have to decide this together."

"I would love to take them. They are ten and five. He said that they are malnourished, as well as unloved. Or so they seem to think. I believe he wishes them to be brought to us as soon as possible." Renie nodded and sat down on the living room's only other seat, a couch that matched the one he was in. "We will need to buy more furniture. Hire some staff to help us. I know very little about two boys in the same household, but I'm willing to learn."

"I know next to nothing about children. I want them here, but it will be a learning curve for us all." Arryn nodded. "Did he happen to mention how many children we are having, while he was at it?"

"Just the one. He could tell us the sex too if we wished, but I didn't ask Him." He waited for her to say more and when she didn't, he continued. "I doubt they know any more about each other than we do them. I was thinking we'd give them separate rooms, yet close in case they needed each other."

"Adjoining rooms. They can be shut if they want, but I think they'll want to be together. If for no other reason than to talk about us." Arryn remembered a charge that he'd had that talked about his parents a great deal with his little sister. "Maybe we can talk Kip into helping us out. He's not much older than our son is."

Arryn loved the sound of that. Our son. She was going to be a great mother, and he was going to enjoy watching her grow large with their next child. He was startled out of his thoughts when a very nicely dressed woman placed a tray in front of him.

"Her name is Cara. She's been sent to take care of the household for us." Arryn nodded to her and then looked at Renie when she continued. "I'm guessing that someone else thinks we're going to need help as well. I don't suppose you can tell me if she's a retired protector too?"

"She is. I've only seen her once in all my years working. I had thought her gone to sleep, but I can see that she will be good for us." He ate one of the cookies on the tray. "And these are good. The boys will love her for them alone."

As soon as Cara left them, Boss appeared in the room. He only sat down a moment before he stood again. Arryn thought that something had happened and he was ready to go to battle for him. But he only said that he needed them both to listen.

"The older boy's name is Gavin and he is well, but the younger one, Kelly...he has been taken to the hospital." Renie asked him which one as she reached for her jacket. "I'm sorry to say this, and I will swear to you that I never meant for this to happen, but they will not allow you to take Kelly without the proper paperwork."

"Which is?" Boss smiled at her and she shook her head. "You're slick, I'll give you that. Is he really sick or is this another one of your tricks?"

"I fear he might not make it."

~~~

Renie looked down at the tiny little guy. He'd been hurt badly and her heart twisted when she thought of how much the two boys had suffered...more than she ever had. But her mother had never beaten her to the extent that he'd been.

His left arm was broken, his right had been twisted so much that it had been dislocated from the socket. It was in place now, but when he woke—if he woke—he'd be in a great deal of pain. Both of his legs had been broken as well, run over by the car that his mother had been driving. She had decided that if the contract between her and Jonas was void, then so would the child be. But it was his little head that had them all worried more than anything.

"The surgeon has cut two holes in his skull to relieve the pressure from the swelling. I can't tell you yet what kind of damage has been done to him, but there will be some." Renie asked the doctor if he might die. "Should he make it thought the next forty-eight hours then he has a chance. But I'm sorry to say that I don't hold out much hope for it. Had he been in better shape physically then he would have no problem pulling through. But I think it has been days, if not weeks, since he's eaten a proper meal."

"He'll live, and when he does, he'll never be hungry again." He had only nodded at her and taken her to sit by Kelly's bed. Boss's sudden appearance wasn't a surprise to her.

"He will have problems should things come to pass as they are now." She couldn't speak past the pain in her heart. "I'm sorry, Reyna. I truly am. I had hopes of him coming to you happy and free of this. But the contract forbade me from seeing him until she had harmed him. I am truly sorry."

"Can You heal him? Make him whole?" He didn't answer her and she looked at Him with blurry eyes. "Please? I don't want him to hurt any more. And short of him dying, I know that You can help him."

"I can. But it will...nothing is without a price, my child. He will come to me as a protector when the time is right. It is the only way I can help him." Renie cried. "You have only to say the word and I will do what I can."

"I can't make that decision for him. It's...that should be his, don't You think? I'm not saying that he won't want to work for You, but to be a protector is something that I think he should decide." Boss said nothing. "I love them already, as You knew that I would. And I want the best for them. Gavin is so...he's broken, but we can help him. He thinks we're going to put him in the system if Kelly doesn't make it."

"Why would he think that?" Renie said nothing and Boss nodded. "I see. Someone has spoken to him about that. His mother no doubt. I will take care that he knows differently." She told him no, that it was their responsibility. "As it should be."

"I'm so sorry, but I can't do it. I'm sure that Arryn would agree with me. But I've had enough things done for me while growing up that I can't do that to my own children." When Boss stood up, she thanked Him. "You will watch over him, won't you? All of us?"

"Forever." He touched His hand to the child's small chest and moved toward the door this time. He turned to look at her after saying her name softly. "I have married you both. The paperwork is filed and should anyone ask, you have adopted them as of this morning. A fitting birthday gift from me, I think."

Her birthday…it was now, as of twenty minutes ago. As she reached for Kelly's hand, Arryn came into the room with her. Gavin, he told her, was at Dusty and Galin's house for now. They sat with Kelly until the nurses told them they were taking him to x-ray again.

After he was gone, she sat in the chair again and tried to wrap her mind around this day. She thought for sure that if someone told her a few months ago that she'd be married, have wings, and be the mother to two boys with a child on the way, she would have laughed in their face.

"I have hired two more people. They won't be staying on, but will help with the furniture in the house. Kip said that he'd help with the boys' rooms, but he has no idea what to tell you because he had so little when he was growing up." Renie had forgotten about that. "Dusty said that she was going to design the rooms for us. Not the furniture, but the walls and things. It's something that she's getting into. And I hope you don't mind, but I told them of the baby."

Renie told Arryn about what Boss had said. "If you think I spoke too soon, let me know. You know more about being a protector than anyone I know. And if you think it's the best way, then I will stand beside you on it."

"No. I think it's the best you could have done for him. I think being a protector is a grand job and I loved it dearly, but you're right. We can't make that decision for him." The nurse came into the room and looked at them before going out again. When she returned a few seconds later, Arryn asked her what was going on.

"The young boy, has he come in here?" Arryn looked at Renie, then at the nurse again. "He was on the table and we were about to shoot the film when he just…he got up."

"Got up how?" The nurse only stared at Renie when she asked. "What do you mean, he just got up? You said that his legs were broken. His ribs too, if I remember correctly. People with broken bones just don't get up."

"I just don't know."

Arryn moved to the door when she did. They were both standing in the hall when a little boy came toward them, looking for all the world like he knew just where he was going. When he stopped in front of Renie, she dropped to her knees and stared at him.

"Hello." Renie nodded at him. "He said that I should find you first. And I was to tell you that…I was to tell you that…." He grinned at her. "He said you made the right pick."

Renie wasn't sure what he meant and looked at Arryn. He was looking just as confused as she was. When asked his name, the little boy said that he was Kelly, but no one had told him his last name since he'd been little.

"We'll have to figure that out as well." As soon as she stood up, he put his hand in hers. Renie looked at Arryn as she continued. "We're going to be your parents. Okay?"

Kelly nodded and said that the other man had told him that too. "I'm really hungry. Do you think I could have something to eat? A burger if it's not too much. I don't have any money, but I can work for you."

"Sure. Would you like to...? Well, I don't know if we can take you home yet. There might be some questions on how you were nearly...well, there might be a few questions." The doctor that had been treating Kelly came down the hall. He said hi to them and asked if they had any questions. "About what?"

"He's got a nasty bump on his head from falling, but I'm sure you know how boys are. He's just fine. I'd just make sure that you pamper him a little more and let him and his brother have some fun time but quiet time. He'll be ready for school again in a few days." Renie looked at Arryn when he stood beside her. "Mr. and Mrs. Advocate, we see this sort of thing all the time. Little boys falling on the playground and the school overreacting. I'm not saying that their overreaction wasn't a good thing, but in this case, it was all right. Kelly here is going to be just fine."

As he moved away from them, telling them that he was going to sign off on his discharge papers now, Renie felt like something had been sucked out of her. Leaning back on Arryn, she held onto Kelly's hand.

"My name is Kelly Advocate?" She told him she thought so. "Cool. I like it. Can we go to your house now? I'm really tired."

"I think that's an excellent idea, son." Arryn picked him up and held him as he held her hand. "Come on, Mom. Let's go home."

As they left the hospital, Arryn was talking to Kelly. Renie had no idea how they'd gotten to the hospital, and was surprised when Arryn led them to a large SUV. After Kelly was strapped in, she closed the door and reached for Arryn. He held her tightly until she lifted her head and looked up at him.

It had taken them nearly two hours to get the papers signed and then another three to figure out what to dress Kelly in. Apparently, they had cut all his clothing off when he was brought in. Arryn had to make a run to Walmart to pick him up some clothing and shoes. It was just going on lunch time now.

"Pizza. Could we stop for pizza?" He told her anything. "Tomorrow we can start on a proper diet, but pizza for my birthday sounds really good. Don't you think?"

"It sounds perfect." As they drove home, she called the house. Ms. Cara told them that she'd take care of having dinner delivered for them, and that the young master had been brought home as well. Mr. Gavin was presently in his room looking around. Ms. Cara said that she'd go shopping for more food later. After she hung up, Renie turned and looked at her son in the back seat. He was sleeping soundly and with a smile on his face. Renie was happy as she'd ever been.

And when she arrived at the house, it was a surprise to her to find not just the Mystics and protectors there, but Boss and Michael as well. But it was the cake and all the flowers on it that had her bawling like a baby when she was told to blow out the candles. Renie would never not celebrate her birthday again if she had friends like this.

"I love you guys." Everyone hugged her and told her that she was loved as well. Renie wondered if they really knew how much they meant to her, and decided that she'd work on that as well.

Chapter 12

The line at the bank wasn't that long, but Arryn wasn't really concerned with how long it was taking them to shuffle the patrons through. He was more concerned with how long it was taking the bank manager to come and talk to them. He'd been told over an hour ago that they were waiting.

Riss and Valyn had come with them. Renie was looking calm and had her files on her lap like she had done this sort of thing many times. Kala was at home with her boys as well as Gavin, who had to wait another week before he could begin classes because they were waiting on the results of his placement testing. Kelly was in school, and Judith was going to get him should this run over…and it was looking more and more like it would.

"Mrs. Advocate? Mr. Grimmer will see you now." When Renie stood, the rest of them did as well. The woman who had come to get her stepped back. "I'm sorry. I just…he thinks that he is only seeing her."

"Where she goes, we go." The woman nodded but looked nervous when Valyn put his hand on her shoulder. "When you take us into his office, I want you to clear out your desk and sit quietly until I tell you that you can leave."

"I can do that." As she led them to the door to the bank president, Arryn asked Valyn what he had done.

"I just made sure first of all that she wasn't a part of this…which she is not. She's wondered about the money he seems to be spending, but never asked. She needs this job." Arryn asked him what else. "She's going to come and work for me. As my cook. It's been her dream to work in a big house and I'm going to let her help me out. There is no reason for her to be unemployed when the bank closes down, right?"

"But you don't like people." Valyn looked at Renie as she moved to have a seat, then looked back at him. There was something there, but Arryn never got a chance to ask him when the banker started speaking.

"I don't know what this is about, but I thought that I was meeting with the new teller we hired. You should know that I don't care for this show of whatever you think this might be. You might have just lost yourself this job." Renie said nothing as two more chairs were placed in front of the big desk. "What is the meaning of this?"

"I'm not your new teller. In fact, the rest of the tellers are being led out by the police even as we speak. They're going to be questioned, but I doubt any of them know what someone at this bank has been doing. If they do, then they too will be arrested." He asked her what she was talking about. "Arrested. You know the meaning of the word. To be seized or taken into custody. Jailed. And in the case of the person skimming money from accounts, prison."

"For what? I demand that you leave here this moment or I'll be calling the police. You've no right to come in here and accuse me of anything." She told him that she'd not accused him of anything. Yet. The door opened again, and a man that Arryn had only met today came in and stood in front of the door. "Who is this? Your gunman? Get out of my office. I have a business schedule today."

As he reached for his phone, Valyn stood up and put his hand on it. Arryn was sure that it wouldn't work for him when he sat back down, but it was funny to watch the man's face. He was scared and getting more scared by the second. Renie put the first sheath of papers on his desk.

"These are the bank statements for Jellies, Jams and Preserves. You might also have it on your books as JJ&P. Or maybe it's marked as client number twelve." Mr. Grimmer didn't even pick the file up, but it didn't stop Renie. "She is number twelve in a longer list of names and clients that this bank, or someone that works here, has been scamming, isn't she?"

"You're barking up the wrong tree there, girl. You should really have some facts before you start spouting things you don't know about." Renie smiled and continued, only to be cut off again. "I'm going to only tell you once more to get out of my office before I call the police."

"They're here, as I have told you. And buddy, your threats are nothing compared to what I've been through lately. I've looked in the face of real evil, and you are nothing but a blip on my computer." She handed him the next file. "This is Strategize Yourself. It's an advertising firm that deals with huge clients with names like Sweet and a few others. She also works with JJ&P as their advertising firm. She's on your list as number ten. I'm not sure how the numbering system works, but I have them all now."

Mr. Grimmer leaned back in his chair but looked nervous. She had him; it was only a matter of him just coming clean. And Renie had assured them all, including the federal agent at the door, that he would come clean.

"The next client that has been scammed is Riss Trainer. He and his lovely wife, Kala, opened their account with nearly fifty million dollars. But the bank manager at the local level told them that they'd have to spread out their money should they want it to be covered. He's a very smart man." Grimmer said that all of his employees were smart. "Not as smart as you, are they? Never mind. The next four accounts, all numbered in order of date of the accounts opening, were Galin and Dusty McGee, Agon and Judith Guardian, and last but not least is Valyn Savior. Now, this is where you...or I mean someone here...messed up. They didn't just skim this money over a period of time, they took out a large chunk of it right at the first. Then they had the nerve to charge him a finder's fee for a house that was sold to him. I had to look that up. Banks aren't allowed to charge a broker's fee on houses that are on their books. I don't know why, but there you have it."

"Broker's fees are fees that can be charged when we help a client find a house to buy. It is perfectly legal." Renie shook her head at Grimmer. "How the hell would you know anything about this? Are you a banker?"

"No. But I do know how to look things up. And on all the websites that I looked on, it says so long as there is at least five hundred dollars in a personal account and a thousand in a business account at all times, there will be no fees. Not for checks cashed, nor any business fees for taking credit cards. Yet at this bank, at this office, the accounts are being charged not only fees, but very large ones. Mr. Collier, the manager at the local level, has taken off the charges for the house and all the other charges that were incurred to these accounts, just so you know. He was appalled that they were there in the first place." That got Grimmer's attention. "Oh, and you should write him a little note when you have time. He has been most helpful in having all the money returned to the accounts. It was with his help that I was able to trace the IP address to this office. I mean, this particular office."

"What do you mean, returned to the accounts? All those fees are legal. I can show you where we have instituted that new policy recently." Mr. Grimmer reached for a pamphlet on his desk, only to stare at Arryn when he stood up. Arryn was glad he could be a part of this. When he opened his notes, Arryn winked at Renie before speaking to Grimmer.

"There were seven off shore accounts. The first five were easy enough to trace back to this office, the last two had been set up from another address, and that was traced back to your home address…this time a physical one, not just a computer one. Is someone there using a computer that is in your office?" Grimmer shook his head slowly. "No one thought so, but we did need to ask. You live alone and have no housekeeper that we could find. You do have a service that comes in once a week to wipe up, but they cannot enter your office. You make sure that it's locked at all times. Isn't that right, Mr. Grimmer?"

"How did you…? You can't know this. Are you spying on me?" Arryn told him that someone was, at all times. When Grimmer moved to his computer, Jack Spencer, the agent, moved to stand right behind him. Arryn watched as Grimmer moved his fingers across the keyboard quickly before he leaned back in his chair. "It's gone. All of it. You really did find the accounts, didn't you?"

"As I have said, it's all been returned to the accounts you took it from." When Spencer told Grimmer to stand up, he staggered slightly when he complied. But it was the look that he gave Renie that had Riss and Valyn move with Arryn to stand in front of her. His hatred was palpable. Cuffs were put on the man as his rights were being read, and Spencer laughed when Grimmer tried to get away from him.

"Why did you do this to me?" Renie asked him what he meant. "This. You know just what I'm talking about. You stole my money. I had great plans for that money. I was going to make a difference with it. This bank prides itself on making differences in other people's lives, and I was going to use some of that for that very reason."

"I'm sure you were. But the money wasn't yours in the first place. And the people you stole it from had plans for their money as well. It was you who were the thief, Mr. Grimmer. You stole from them. I merely replaced it." When Spencer started to finish reading Grimmer his rights, Arryn moved to stand beside Renie. He could feel her fear and pain.

When Grimmer and Spencer were gone, three men came in to gather things off the desk and in the files. Valyn went to talk to the woman he'd put on hold in the other office. Arryn simply held onto Renie.

"He's going away for a long time, I think." He agreed with her. "I did this to him. I mean, I know it was his doing, but I caught him. And as much as I hated making him realize it, I really enjoyed it."

"Good." They both turned to look at Spencer when he spoke. "I've spoken to a few of my colleagues while I've been working with you, and we'd like to hire you. As a consultant. I know that your time is valuable and we'd never interfere with that, but you could work from home and on as many projects as you want. Right now we have a back log of about two hundred, give or take a few more hundred."

"You mean doing the things I did here?" He nodded, then shook his head. "You're not very clear. I thought you guys were like the smartest people in the world."

"Yeah, if that were only true. The bad guys — in this case, the cyber bad guys — are smarter than us and getting smarter by the day. Had you not found this, we would never have known a thing." He handed them both a card. "Call me if you have any questions. And I'm serious when I tell you that you could help us out a great deal. And a lot of people like the ones you helped here would be very grateful as well."

After he left them, they met the rest of their group at the car. It was lunch time and then after that, they were headed home. Judith was called and told what happened, and then she said she'd call the rest of them. She also said that Gavin was having a great time with her and Kala and the babies. Arryn just wanted to get back to his own family.

~~~

"I can't do that." Renie nodded at Gavin. He really was a great kid, but he was as lost over what to do with her as she was him. And getting him to open up was harder still. "You don't have to spend that kind of money on me. I'm fine with what I gots."

"Have. You're fine with what you have. But you have to study, and wouldn't it be better if you had your own computer?" He didn't so much as blink an eye in response to her question. "Look, I have nine laptops, and eight of them are just sitting in the boxes. The FBI is going to supply me with what I need, but—"

"The FBI? You work for them?" She nodded and turned away. It was the first time he'd been animated about anything she'd said to him. "What do you do? Kill the bad guys? Do you get a gun too?"

"I'm sort of a boring kind of agent. Well, not really an agent so much as a colleague to a bunch of agents. They'll be coming here some. I'll make sure you can meet them if you want." He nodded vigorously. "And what I do is find the bad guys through my computer work."

"You can find them with a computer?" Gavin eyed the one in her hand. "Did you use that one to find them? Is it the one you used to catch him?"

"It is one of the ones I used." Renie put it out to him and he stepped back. "I could show you how I do it. I mean, if you wanted to see it. I love what I do."

Gavin wanted the computer. And not only that, she could tell he wanted her to help him with it. But she was thinking of what Kip had told her. Don't push. It would only make him want to back off more.

"I guess it would be nice for homework. I know you won't let me have the Internet and all. It's too expensive." She told him the whole house was hooked up, as was the wireless printer that she had for him. "Why are you doing this? You know that in a few days, you're going to want to get rid of us again."

"Why would you say something like that?" He shrugged. "I'm not going to get rid of you. Not ever. You're my son. You and Kelly are going to live here for the rest of your lives."

"Kelly is cute. I'm not." She look at him, really looked at the kid. "I know that you only took me because that man asked you to."

"You need a haircut. And some cloths that fit you." Renie asked him to turn for her. "And some boots and shoes. How old are those you have on?"

"They were in the box at the shelter we were at before you came to get us." Renie nodded, put the computer on the desk, and told him to come with her. They were nearly down the stairs when he asked her where they were going.

"The school first, to get Kelly. He gets out in…well, it's too early for that. Why don't you and I go to the computer store? I need a few things there, and I got your school results back too. Did you know that they want to put you in eighth grade already? I was going to talk to you about that but I forgot. I have a horrible memory when I'm working." She gathered up her purse and her jacket. "After we go to the computer store, we can pick up Kelly and have a mall shopping spree. Haircuts, then we can have dinner. Maybe Arryn will be done by then and—"

"Hang on." Renie turned to look at Gavin when he cut her off. "You don't have to do this. No one is going to care if I have a haircut and if I have boots that fit. I'm not sure why you think…it's not nice of you to tease me with this stuff then take it away from me. My mom did that to me all the time. I won't take it so you can take it back."

"But I care that you have shoes and a coat. I think a haircut would go a long way to making you feel better, and I'm not going to take things back from you like she did. Not ever." She got into her new car and hoped that he'd join her. When he got in the front seat she felt like a major victory had been won. "I need some paper and stuff. I have your list too. You can get all that while I haggle a good price on five printers. You get it all too, and whatever else you need for your room. If you don't, then I'll get it in pink or with some daisies."

"You're going to do this no matter what, huh?" She told him she was. "Why? I'm pretty sure that you don't care what other people think, not about yourself anyway. I mean...you're pretty tough and you have a...I was gonna say mean streak...about you, but that's not right either. It's more of a fuck you kind of thing."

"It is. Don't use that language again, but I'd very much like for you to adopt the same kind of attitude too. It's going to get you far in life." As she started the car up she thought of all the things she wanted to do for these guys and was excited about it. But Boss had told her that it was important to talk to him about why he was with her and Arryn. "Gavin, I'm really sorry about your life. Did you know that the same thing happened to me? My mother sold me so that she could live forever too."

"She said that I was worthless." She heard the pain in his voice and the anger. "I'm not worthless. I can do some stuff."

"You can do a lot of things if you want. But I want you to trust me when I tell you that Arryn and I are thrilled to death to have you and Kelly here with us. I never...I thought by this time I'd be in hell. Not just there, but a playmate to some evil demon that made the same deal with my mom that he did with yours."

"You mean sex." She nodded. "I won't have sex with a man. No matter what he does to me. I will never ever do that."

She knew that he'd been sexually abused. The doctors had told them that while he had, Kelly had not. Renie also knew that he was going to need help with this sooner rather than later, more help than she could give him. As they drove to the first stop, she talked about the things that she needed and asked him what he might need.

"This list has a lot of stuff on it. I mean a lot. What if we just got some of it now and then later, if I really need it, we get it then?" She told him that he needed it all and that she could afford it. "It might cost like fifty bucks. That's a lot of money."

"It is. But I work for the government now and they're paying me really well." As they got out of the car, something occurred to her. "You want a job? It won't be much, but I'll pay you every week so long as you do it."

Gavin backed away from her and asked her what it was. Renie wanted to reach out and grab him and hold him, but she knew that it would be the wrong thing to do. He did not like to be hugged.

"Well, first you can load the dishwasher after dinner. Kelly can unload it later. But what I really need is someone to help me in my new office. It's not far from the school, and you can come by afterwards and work. I need someone to take out the trash after you shred it, and then run the sweeper once a week. I'll pay you thirty bucks a week." He didn't look like he believed her. "In cash of course. And so long as you save some of it, you can do whatever you want with the rest."

"How much do I have to save?" She asked him what a good figure was. "Will I need to pay you rent? Or for my food?"

"Good heavens no. That's part of being our family. If you want something extra in the house, let Ms. Cara know. She said you don't care for broccoli. Well, we're alike in that, neither do I."

"I can save half. Can I put it in a bank? One that you can't get to?" She told him she didn't know if he was old enough to have his own account, but she'd never touch his money. "She said that too. I want to buy me a car someday."

"Good. You can put as much or as little as you want each week in the bank, and I'll never touch it. If you trust someone more than me, you can ask them to co-sign with you." He told her she'd be all right. "Thank you."

As she put in her order for the new office, she told Arryn what she'd said to Gavin and what he'd said to her. He said it was probably the best thing to do, let him make some of his own decisions. Arryn told her, too, that he'd love to meet them for dinner. But he wanted a real dinner, not burgers.

I think they should decide. I'm not sure how many pizza's they've had in their life, but I have a feeling it was a lot. Did you see the way that they ate that meatloaf last night? Like it was the biggest steak they'd ever had. He said that it was pretty good. *Ms. Cara said she was going to lay in more supplies today. I guess it's a good thing we both have good jobs. We're going to need it to feed them.*

It took them nearly two hours to get everything they needed. Gavin got everything on his list, and even let her buy him a desk. The one in his room was small, too small for a computer, and instead of the laptop, she got him a computer. Kelly could use the laptop for his homework. By the time they were at the school to get Kelly, both of them were starved, but the teacher needed to see her about something.

"We've had a talk with Kelly today on his lying to everyone. I understand that he's not your son." Renie took an immediate dislike to Mrs. Summer, the principal. "He's telling everyone that will listen that his mother sold him to the devil and you saved him. We can't have that kind of disruption in the class room, Mrs. Advocate. Even if he's not your son, you should teach him manners."

"Disruptions? And if you say that he's not my son again I will have you brought up on charges. I'm not sure what, but I'm sure that I can dig something up." The woman huffed at her and said something low under her breath. "What did you just say to me?"

"I said that no wonder he's such a problem child. And it's only his first week, too. That one, I'm sure that once we get him, he's going to be just as bad. I've read his file." Renie saw red and her heart was pounding when she asked Gavin to step into the hall. When he said that he wanted to stay, Renie turned to the woman again.

"You ever talk about my sons like that again in front of them and I will hurt you in ways that will haunt you for the rest of your life. So help me I will. As for my sons being a problem, well, you don't have to worry about that either. I'm going to have you dismissed as soon as I leave here. To think…I cannot believe that Judith thought that this was going to be a good fit for my children."

"Judith Guardian?" The change in the woman was astonishing. "Oh well, you should have said you were friends with her. I'll have to check it out, of course, but we could not run this place without her donations. She and her money have made a big difference in the amount of money we have to spend yearly on simple supplies that the downtrodden can't seem to afford because of the money they spend on cigarettes and alcohol."

Renie reached for Judith, and in seconds she was coming into the office with her. Mrs. Summer stood up and gushed over Judith as if she were the best thing in the world. As she made over her friend, Renie told her what she'd said. As they were being seated, Gavin too, drinks were offered.

"You have a problem with my godsons? I assure you that they are the best of boys." Mrs. Summer started in on how it was all a misunderstanding and that she had spoken out of turn. "You have. And I won't have it. As of this moment, I'm finished with you and this school. And if your superiors would like for me to explain why I'm no longer funding this institution, then by all means, have them call me." Judith stood up and so did Renie. "And if you ever say a bad thing about my godsons again, or their mother and father, I will have you put into a world of hurt. Do you understand me?"

Nodding, Mrs. Summer tried again to say it was simply a misunderstanding. The three of them left the office and gathered up Kelly and his things. The little guy was so upset that he was sobbing when they got to the car. Gavin held him while they just sat in the car; Renie was too upset to drive safely. Judith asked if she was all right.

"No, I'm not all right. That woman called my sons a disruption. She called them downtrodden and liars. Then when I mentioned you, it was as if a cloud was lifted from her meanness and she was suddenly all goody two shoes." Gavin laughed in the back seat. "You think she was funny?"

"No. You are. And I gotta tell you, I will never think again that you don't want us. You sure did put a crimp in her day." He laughed again and shook his head. "I have never seen a woman so fired up for me before. It was amazing. I'm never going to mess with you."

"See that you don't." He laughed again and so did Kelly this time. "Thank you. I feel better now. Are you guys ready to go school shopping? And we'll have to find us a new school too. I think private this time. I don't know if they would be any less bigoted, but we'll make sure they know what is what before you can go."

By the time the three of them were at the mall, Judith having gone back to her own shop, they were all feeling pretty good. Even Gavin was in a much better mood when she told him that he was going to get a wash and a cut, not just a cut. Things were looking up, she thought.

Chapter 13

Valyn moved out of the house and into the yard. It wasn't that he didn't love the house he had purchased, but it felt…crowded. He knew that the only other person in the place was his new cook, Janie Preston, but he didn't like people. Why he had hired her was beyond him. As he made his way to the deck furniture that Riss and Kala had gotten him as a housewarming present, he wasn't really surprised to see Michael there.

"I should like to have a conference with you, please?" Valyn nodded and sat down on the bench that came with the set. Michael was pacing, and for the moment, Valyn let him. He was outside and he felt calmer for the moment. "When should you be back on rotation?"

"Not for another two weeks. I'm exhausted, so please don't ask me to go so soon. I know that you're short, but I'm really tired." Michael nodded and continued to move back and forth.

"I know nothing about houses." It was a strange statement, even for Michael. "They are…how does one go about getting one? Where would one begin to look? Where would one begin to look into a lister to help with this? And my funds have been turned over to hard cash, she called it, but how do I know if I have enough?"

"Listing. I'm sure you have plenty of cash, Michael, we all do. Have you talked to Renie about helping you? She helped me. I nearly purchased the wrong kind of house." They both turned and looked at his home.

If asked, he would have said that this house was wrong for him as well. There were nine bedrooms on the upper floor, with three bathrooms and a master suite on the second floor, along with an office with an attached library. The ground level had a sprawling living room, huge dining room, and a kitchen that he'd been told could accommodate a hundred guests. There was also a family room as well as a rec room, but he had no idea what that was used for. The entire thing was surrounded by a covered deck that had a hot tub he'd yet to fill, as well as a pool that looked big enough for the Olympics to be held in. For a single man that didn't care for company, the house was not suitable. He'd asked for a large house to roam in, but he'd not thought of how big this one was until he'd already purchased it.

"I need to invest, I was told. Renie has...did you know that she is holding classes at the compound? She was called away today when the Federacies needed her, but she said she would return tomorrow." Valyn corrected him again. "Feds. They are most scary, are they not?"

"Not if you're being a good boy, they're not." Valyn looked out over the expansive yard and wondered again what he was doing there. "Am I next on the list?"

"List? There is another list that I have no idea of?" Valyn clarified for him. "Wedded list? I'm not sure that there is one. I know that Boss has His secrets, but as far as a wedded list, I don't think I've heard of it."

Michael was a terrible liar. He flushed when he did it and he wouldn't look at you in the face, just as he was doing right now. Valyn stood up and started toward the smaller man. Michael backed away from him.

"There is no reason for you to get huffy with me. I know not what He does until He tells me. *In good time.* You know that He says that to me more than He does anyone? And *you shall see.* I see nothing. It is as if He likes having me fumbling in the dark." Valyn stopped moving toward him. "I cannot reason with Him either. He will do as He pleases, to whomever He pleases, no matter what I say to Him."

"I don't want to be wedded. I cannot stand to be with people, and I'm pretty sure that if He were to find me a bride, she'd expect me to be close to her." Michael nodded and smiled at him. "Would you please tell Him that it would be wrong of Him to hurt a female like this? I'm not worthy of His time."

"Not worthy? I don't understand that statement. Not worthy how?" Valyn said nothing as he took his seat again. "You must explain to me what that means. Because I'm thinking I have the definition of it wrong. To be not worthy is something that means to me that you are beneath consideration. And that cannot be how you feel about yourself."

Valyn wanted to change the subject, but felt if he could make Michael understand him, then Boss would as well. It was a long shot, he knew, but he had to try to make them both back off from this.

"I've been around for a long time. Seen things, heard things that most people...humans...would not think twice about. But it's day after day for me. Not just from the people that I am to watch over, but the people—humans again—that interact with them. Hate and despair. There is so much of it around that it saddens my heart." Michael said that not all people were like that. "No. I've seen Riss and Kala together with their children. I've observed the way that Galin and Dusty have come together in such happiness as well. Agon is as happy as I've ever seen him with his new family. And though they are only starting out, Renie and Arryn seem to be the happiest of all of them."

"You don't wish to have such happiness, Valyn?" Valyn shook his head. "Because you believe yourself to be unworthy, is that why?"

"It is. I'm not…I'm not happy." Michael's sharp intake of breath made Valyn know that he'd shocked the man. "I've not been happy for a very long time. Even since before Riss was thinking of ending his life. I considered it long before that. I think I would feel better to be cut off from all mankind, even the protectors."

"You have not told Boss yet, have you?" Valyn told him that he'd been working up to it. "I would not wait much longer. Should you…should you be this unhappy, there might be something that he can do to help you."

"Not a bride." Michael said nothing. "A woman in my life will be as unhappy with me as I would be with her. She would be left alone for great lengths of time. I cannot be a mate to anyone when I do not even care for myself."

"I am sorry, Valyn. If he has chosen you a bride, she will…I feel you are doing yourself and her a disjustice in thinking that you'd have nothing to offer her. Or her to offer you in return. I do know that he has a woman in mind for Tholan, but that is not even in the realm of things to happen right now." Valyn corrected him without thinking. "Injustice. It would most assuredly be just that if you were to say no to this."

Long after Michael left, Valyn sat on his deck. When the moon was full in the sky, he made his way to his new bedroom and laid out on the bed. He was sure that his life was about to change, and not in a way that he wanted. Rolling to his side, he pulled out the small charm that he'd had since he'd first become a protector. It was given to him so long ago that the face of the child that had handed it to him was a faded memory. But the day wasn't.

His charge was at the beach. It was a sunny bright day, and there were many people on the sand. Few of them would venture into the water, and those that did ran out quickly, for it was still early April. The child that he was watching was one such child.

"I can see you." Valyn had looked around, trying to see who he was speaking to. "I've seen you ever since I was first born. And I know you have wings, too."

Valyn looked at the boy then as he continued to build a castle in the cold wet sand. When he glanced up at him then went back to his work, Valyn knew a kind of fear that he'd never experienced before or since.

"Why do you think it is you can see me? When no one else can?" The stone in his hand now was handed to him by the child. "Thank you. But I cannot take this."

"I can see you because I'm going to die. Soon." Valyn said nothing. He knew it too. It was why they were here on this day instead of when it was warmer. "They wanted me to have a good day before I went back to the hospital."

"They did." Valyn had seen no reason to lie to him. "You are ready to go, I know this. But your parents are not. They are hurting badly."

"I know." The castle was taking shape now; the boy was working hard to make sure that his mom and dad thought he was really enjoying himself. "I hurt too. And

I'm really tired. I just want to go to sleep and let you take me away."

Valyn nodded and watched him closely. He could see it now, how much it was costing him to play as he was. All these years later they would have been able to cure him. A procedure to make his lungs work better would have saved his life, but then it was not available yet.

"I think they need this time." The boy nodded. "You know that they love you, don't you? That they'd do anything to make you better if they could."

"I know." He sat back on his heels and stared at him. "But I'm ready now. I think...can you take me now? Not later, when you're supposed to, but right here on this pretty place? I want to go."

Boss appeared before them, His wings spread out behind Him in a way that sheltered them from the sun. The boy, of course, couldn't see Him, not yet at any rate, but Valyn did. And he knew why He was there.

"Is this something that you wish as well, Valyn? He is to die regardless of the date on the calendar. Today or the day after, it matters little in his time." Valyn had looked at his young charge as he struggled to breathe under the pain. When he nodded, Boss nodded as well. "Take him now, while his parents are looking on. It will be better for them, I think. To know that his last day was a happy one." Boss disappeared as quickly as He had come to them. Valyn looked at the child, so riddled with pain and sadness, and put out his hand.

"Would you like to have them closer to you? To say goodbye?"

The boy glanced at his parents, who waved at him, and his mother blew him a kiss.

"No. Now. While they look. I think…they'll be sad for a time, but they'll be happy I'm no longer hurting." When he put out his hand, Valyn put his in the smaller one. His smile made Valyn think of angels and snowy wings. "Oh yes. Oh yes. This feels so much better."

It was the last time that Valyn had ever let someone come close to him. No one touched his heart again after that, not even the people that he worked with daily. At least until recently. When the man that he'd been sent to watch over had murdered so many and he'd not been able to stop him.

~~~

"Hot ham on rye, hold the mayo and tomatoes. Fries and burger, American with toasted bun. Hold onions." Jenny put the slip up on the order ring as it was being read back to her by the grill cook. She was headed to the milk shake machine when the door behind her opened and closed. The cool breeze was like a small slice of heaven in the hot assed diner. As the words that seemed as natural to her as breathing started to spill from her lips…*Have a seat, I'll be right with you*…the man pulled out a gun and aimed it at her. The gun firing had her dropping to the floor as it sprayed above her.

The screams made her cover her ears, and a woman begging for her life had her reaching for her cell. It was gone, of course; when you didn't pay the bill, they sort of shut the sucker off. And why carry it around if it wasn't good for anything? And the only other phone was the one in the kitchen, which was currently being shouted into by Jimmy, the cook. He was screaming that they were being robbed, that the man had a gun. Jenny didn't know why, but she doubted that robbery was on this man's mind.

The swinging door to the kitchen opened then swung back and forth as shots were fired in that area. Jimmy's voice, loud and panicky, was cut off when three shots were fired. Jenny tried her best to crawl into the tightest ball she could manage so no one would notice her. It really was a hopeful thought.

"Get up." Jenny looked up at the man who had brought all the terror he could into her tiny piece of the world. "I said to get the fuck up."

"Please don't shoot me." He fired the gun then and shot her in the leg. Jenny screamed at the pain. When he jerked her up off the floor, Jenny stumbled into him and felt the gun in the back of his pants. She grabbed it before she could think how stupid she was. Without any knowledge as to what the fuck she was doing, Jenny pointed the gun at the man who was in front of her.

"Gimme that." She backed from him as she tried to figure out how to get it in her hands correctly. "You're going to die anyways, bitch; you got no reason to make it hard on me."

"You killed them." He looked around, then back at her as if she was pointing out something that he knew. "Why?"

"Don't know. Just got up this morning and decided that I'd kill me a few people, then myself. You give me that gun and I'll make your dying as quick as mine." Shaking her head no, the gun went off. The bullet hit him in the chest and he leaned backwards but did not fall over. He was raising his gun again when she realized that she'd have to pull the trigger again or die now. But she had no idea how she'd done it in the first place.

The scream of sirens made him turn to the front of the diner. Jenny didn't look. She was not just afraid that he'd lunge at her, but she was really trying hard not to look around. There had been blood dripping down off the counter onto her, and she thought that was more than enough for her to see. When she took her eyes off the man long enough to see where her fingers were, he grabbed her and the thing in her hands jumped again. This time the man dropped to the ground.

The police entered then. They were screaming at her to do something, but for the life of her all she could see was that half his face was missing from the chin up, and that his eyes were still opened. As the blood pooled under him, Jenny looked at the man standing to her left. He was wearing wings, her baffled mind told her, but she knew that wasn't right.

"Put the gun on the counter. They won't hurt you if you do." Nodding, she tried to do just what he said but her fingers wouldn't cooperate. "Tell them that you're afraid. Tell them that you're trying to do what they want, but you're terrified he'll get up again."

"Will he get up again?" She looked at the man that she had thought was dead, then at the winged man. "He won't get up, will he?"

The officer that was suddenly there told her no, he was dead. He put his hand over hers and told her that he had her. Nodding, Jenny watched him pry her fingers off the gun like it was being done to someone else. When he had it free, he asked her to back away.

"He said that he got up this morning and wanted to kill somebody." She looked around at the bodies. "I think he did it."

The bubble of laughter had her putting her hand over her mouth. It was then that she noticed that she was covered in blood. As she started for the kitchen to wash up, the officer told her not to move.

"I have to wash my hands. Jimmy, the cook, will be really upset with me when he sees what a mess I am." Jenny knew that she was babbling, but her head didn't seem to want to work with her mouth. And there was so much pain in her leg that she thought that she'd pulled something again. "I just want to wash up, and then I'll need to get the mop."

"You'll need to see a doctor first." She asked him why. "You've been shot, love. Did he do that to you? Is that why you shot him?"

"I shot him? I don't think so. I don't know how to use a gun. But if I did, I think I'd shoot him because he was going to kill me and nothing else. He said that he'd make it quick if I gave him his gun back. But to be honest with you, as sucky as my life has been up until now, dying quick or slow had never occurred to me." Feeling slightly dizzy, she asked if she could have a seat. As she made her way to the stool several more cops came into the room. "Have a seat, I'll be with you in a minute."

She was still giggling when she was led out of the diner. It was colder than she'd thought it was, and she said that to the man who was helping her walk. He only looked at her oddly, then said it was winter.

"I know that. But when I was working, the door opened and...." Something was right there for her to touch on, but she shied away from it. "What happened to me?"

"What do you remember?" She said that it was cold and that the door opened. "Nothing else? Do you remember the man with the gun?"

"Gun? No. You have one." He nodded, but just watched her like she was going to grab it and start kill— "I think something happened. I can almost see it, but I don't...I don't think I want to."

"You're in shock." Jenny didn't say anything because her mind was playing tricks on her. The man with the wings told her that he'd be there with her for a little while longer. But he told her to not talk about him. The officer asked her what her name was.

"Jennifer Hale, but everyone calls me Jenny. I need to lay down, please. I feel kind of sick." Almost as soon as she said it, her belly began to rumble. Someone helped her to lay down, but she sat up before she tossed her cookies. As she tried breathing through it, not puking all over the place, the man with her started to work on her leg.

"What's happened to me?" He asked her if she was allergic to anything. "I don't think so. I can't afford anything so I never use stuff. Maybe some aspirin when I can get it from work, but nothing else. You never told me what happened to...." She felt light, and her body seemed to be crumbing down on itself. As the man with her shot something into her arm, she tried her best to ask him what he was doing. Then there was nothing else.

When Jenny woke again she was in a hospital room. There were people in the room with her; one she knew, the rest she had no idea. The nurse that had been taking her blood pressure asked her how she was feeling, and she told her fine and asked why she was there.

"You're in the hospital. Just out of surgery, as a matter of fact. They removed the bullet from your leg and had to do some repair work too. The doctor will be in soon to talk to you." Jenny didn't say anything but asked when she could go home. "Not for a while yet. I'd say about a week. You have to stay off your leg to make sure it heals."

"I can't be off work for that long. Jimmy will fire me." The nurse nodded and moved away. A man that she didn't know came to stand in front of her, and she thought he looked familiar. Jenny tried to toss the covers off her to get up when she realized how tired she was.

"Miss Hale? My name is Benny Anderson. I'm with the homicide department downtown." She asked him if someone she knew had died. "They told me that you were a little out of it. Did you hit your head when he shot you?"

"I wasn't shot." Mr. Anderson said nothing but pulled a chair to the side of her bed. "I need to go home. I'm not sure what happened, but I have to go to work. There was...I think there was a mess to clean up. Did I drop a tray?"

"No, ma'am. A man by the name of Edward Goodman came into the restaurant yesterday morning. Do you remember that?" Jenny told him that she didn't know anyone by that name. "He came in around noon when the diner was full of people. You were behind the counter."

"I work the counter. I'm good at it." He nodded and smiled at her. "What are you trying really hard not to tell me? I feel like I'm in some sort of movie where there is a mystery but no one knows what it is."

"Mr. Goodman came in to the diner about ten after twelve. He had three hand guns and enough extra ammo to shoot several hundred people. When he came through the door, he shot a woman sitting at the counter, and you screamed and ducked below the camera angles. There were cameras all over the diner, did you know that? Anyway, Jimmy—I'm assuming that's the cook—he called it in, screaming at us that someone had come in shooting the place up to rob you and that everyone was dead. The dispatcher heard the shots then as the phone laid there on the floor; she heard his conversation with you before you killed him." Jenny shook her head. None of this was real. "He shot you in the leg when you wouldn't get up quick enough. Then when he jerked you toward him, you grabbed the gun. The first time you fired at him was a fluke, I think. You seemed as surprised as he was that it went off. As the first officers arrived on scene, they witnessed you—"

"No. Stop." Her head was spinning and she put her hands over her eyes. "I don't know what you're talking about. I didn't shoot anyone. I was working. Today, I was serving breakfast and that's all."

"There were nine people still alive in the restaurant when you killed him. Had you not shot him, we're sure that he would have killed them as well as you before we arrived." Bits of it were coming back to her. Not all, but enough that she knew some of what he was saying was right.

"I'd like to go home please. Can I please go home? Now?" He shook his head and handed her a photo. Jenny turned away from it when she saw the face. "I don't know him. I can...I don't want to remember. All right? I just want to forget."

"I'm sorry, but I need you to remember what happened. I don't want people thinking you were a part of what he did." She asked him who would think that. "Anyone that would think that suing you would get them a big payday."

"Payday? I can't even afford my cell phone to keep it working. I don't have a car, no money in the bank. Every penny I have goes to a credit card company that I never heard of, paying a debt that I didn't incur, and to rent. I only have food in my belly because I get two free meals a day when I work a double, and my tips are split between me and five other waitresses that rarely show up to work but on payday." He told her he was sorry. "I can't afford this. I can't be here, I can't help you, and I certainly don't have any money for this so called payday. I'd very much like to go home."

"If I have to arrest you to get what I want, then I will, but in the meantime, you're going to be here. Do you want me to put a guard outside this room? Or do I need to handcuff you to the bed?" Jenny laid back on the bed. Somewhere in her head she knew that he was treating her wrong, but she was just too tired at the moment to fight with him. Closing her eyes, Jenny heard him telling someone to set a guard on her, and that he was arresting her on suspicion of something. Jenny felt someone touch her hand and looked at the winged man again.

"I'll take care of you." She nodded. "Close your eyes, love. In a little while, you'll understand what I've done for you."

"I want to go home." He nodded. "You're real, aren't you? I mean, you're really here talking to me."

"I am. And soon you'll be with friends. And with a man that will love you above all others." She told him that wasn't going to happen and she thought that he laughed. Her eyes felt heavy and she let them close as something hard and cold was put on her wrist.

About the Author

Kathi Barton, author of the bestselling series Force of Nature, lives in Nashport, Ohio with her husband Paul. In addition to writing full time Kathi likes to spend time with her eight grandkids, three children and three children-in-laws. She writes to relax and have fun.

Her muse, a cross between Jimmy Stewart and Hugh Jackman brings them to life for her readers in a way that has them coming back time and again for more. Her favorite genre is paranormal romance with a great deal of spice. You can visit Kathi on line and drop her an email if you'd like. She loves hearing from her fans. aaronskiss@gmail.com.

Follow Kathi on her blog:
http://kathisbartonauthor.blogspot.com/

www.ingramcontent.com/pod-product-compliance
Lightning Source LLC
Chambersburg PA
CBHW032132170626
46808CB00006B/2196